SON OF CAIN

A Novella

by
John Edgell

Text Copyright © John A. Edgell
All Rights Reserved

A Quick Read Book

REALMS OF LIGHT BOOKS

website
Johnedgell-author.com

email
Jaedgell.author@gmail.com

Dedicated to Sue—helper and encourager.
I am blest to have her as my wife and best friend.

Contents

Prologue   –   page 11

Chapter 1   –   page 13 . . . The Man in Black

Chapter 2   –   page 21 . . . Whisperings of a Soul

Chapter 3   –   page 29 . . . Valley of No Return

Chapter 4   –   page 41 . . . The Enchantress

Chapter 5   –   page 51 . . . The Raven's Cackle

Chapter 6   –   page 55 . . . The Hunter

Chapter 7   –   page 63 . . . Quest for the God

Chapter 8   –   page 69 . . . The Waresman

Chapter 9   –   page 77 . . . Poor Majet

Chapter 10   –   page 87 . . . Vale of Mourning

Chapter 11   –   page 95 . . . Journey's End

Chapter 12   –   page 103 . . Dreadful Dreams

Chapter 13   –   page 109 . . Ol' Noah Was Right

Prologue

"You have driven me from Your presence to be a fugitive and a vagabond in the lands." And God set a mark on Cain.   The Book of Beginnings

Some children are a blessing, others a curse. Adam and Eve wept over Abel. His brother, Cain, sneered. He had killed Abel—mankind's first murder—but no one knew, no one but God.

A voice rumbled from the heavens, "Cain, where is your brother?"

"I don't know," Cain growled. He set his jaw and added, "Am I my brother's keeper?"

"Your brother's blood cries to me from the ground. Now you are cursed, a fugitive and a vagabond you shall be on the earth, a marked man."

Taking a sister sympathetic to his cause, Cain fled from the presence of the Lord to a distant land. He called the place Nod. There he dwelt and multiplied away from the presence of God, cursed and a curse to his progeny.

Chapter 1
The Man in Black

The earth was corrupt before the God, and the earth was filled with violence. The Book of Beginnings

The driving snow's taskmaster howled angrily at the man enshrouded in a heavy black coat with his face withdrawn into the folds of its fur-lined cowl. Snow berries dangled from his huge black stallion's shaggy winter coat. Ice crusted the rider's eyebrows and lids. He strained to see the trail, but visibility on the narrow mountain pass was zero. He reined his steed tight to the high wall and pressed on.

   A shadow passed, and the peculiar squall intensified. Gale force winds worked at casting horse and rider down into white darkness. The driving snow pelted the black coat and wool wraps that protected the man from the frigid mountain air. Undaunted by the hostile weather, the man pressed his heels to the stallion's ribs.

   Timeless hours passed before the intensity of the storm abated. The light beyond the blowing snow began to fade, until finally a surreal undark night encompassed the mountain. The powerful stallion painstakingly plodded upward. When the man came to a cavernous recess reaching back into the escarpment, he turned aside. The black bowels of the mountain swallowed both horse and rider. The clatter of the steed's hooves measured the cavern. The man drew him to silence, and slipped down to the cave floor. The scuffing of the man's feet echoed off the walls of the grotto. His horse snuffled restively. Once again a shadow passed in the night, and the wind began to whisper threats through crack and crevice. The man ignored the night sounds. He struck flint, and sparks nipped at the darkness. A flame flickered to life. Soon a fire crackled and shadows shivered on the icy walls. Smoke swirled upward, worked its way along the ceiling, found a crack and escaped out into the night.

The great black busied itself in an oat bag, while the man curried away its collection of unwanted adornments. With his horse cared for, the man removed a pan from the edge of the fire and fed himself. He leaned against the rock wall, took out a small silver pipe and put it to his lips. A mournful tune harmonized with the eerie howl of the wind. And as the storm calmed, the piper's song died away. The man lowered his flute, pulled his wraps close about and let his eyelids droop shut.

By the time the piper's song was done the small fire had faded to embers. In the recesses of the cave, something stirred. A mannish creature, a troglodyte, protected from the cold only by the hair that covered its body, advanced with soundless step toward the man enfolded in black. The man's steed clicked its hooves and whinnied nervously. The troglodyte hesitated before padding closer. It raised its stone club and with the force of death smashed downward. As the bludgeon fell, the man in black rolled aside, came to his feet, and while the startled cave dweller faltered, the man seized it by the shoulders and rammed its thick skull into the unyielding wall.

The troglodyte fell limp at the man's feet.

The man in black tied the cave dweller hand and foot, and salved the gash left by the jagged wall. He added wood to the fire and sat on the cold stone floor and waited. When the troglodyte finally lifted its head, the man in black saw fear in the creature's overly large eyes. "That's good," the man muttered. He cast the mannish creature a wry smile. The cave dweller grunted and growled in return.

"Do you speak language?" the man gruffed.

The hairy creature glared at the man in black, but held its tongue.

The man stared back. He extended the palms of his hands toward the fire. "All men speak language. Surely you men of the mountains have not lost the ability to speak."

The wild man growled, and snapped meat-ripping teeth at his captor.

The man in black grinned. "Well, whether you speak language or not at least you understand it."

The cave dweller struggled against the ropes that hobbled him, shot the man an angry glare, and hissed, "I kill man from valley! I smash his head with club!"

"So, you do speak language." Watching the creature out the corner of his eye, the man in black tossed a couple of sticks on the fire. "Do you have a name?"

The wild man cursed and spat at his captor. The spit landed on the glowing coals and sizzled into oblivion. The man from the valley leaned an elbow on his knee and cast the cave dweller an icy look. "Feisty brute, aren't you?"

"I no brute. I son of Cain."

"I'll grant that you're a son of Cain, but..." The man wrapped in black let the sentence drop. He returned to his place in the shadows beyond the fire, leaned back against the wall, and studied the troglodyte. After a bit he interrupted the cave's whisperings. "I too am a son of Cain. However, I'm a civilized son, while you're a churl, dear cousin. Your lineage traces to Karg, Cain's bastard son by the harlot Nurga. Karg the Demented, who was driven from Nod by Cain's normal children."

The cave dweller's blank stare indicated he had no idea what the man was talking about. "Son of Cain!" he repeated.

"Well, Son of Cain, my name is Dar'ock."

The wild man muttered something unintelligible and spat again. The spittle fell short of its mark. The man in black shook his head. "I didn't think you'd be particularly impressed. Anyway, wild man, I was told that you cave dwellers are familiar with the enchantress, Deva."

The cave dweller stiffened. Fear sheeted his face. The corner of Dar'ock's mouth twitched upward. "Well, churl, since you're familiar with the enchantress, I'm sure you won't mind taking me to her lair?"

The burly brute's upper lip curled into something halfway between a snarl and a smile, and his eyes glinted with impishness.

"Devilish, but he'll serve my purpose," Dar'ock mumbled to himself, and with a self-satisfied sort of smirk creasing his face, he leaned back, pulled his black coat close about, closed his eyes and went to sleep.

Dar'ock woke at the first trace of dawn, and looked over to where the wild man lay. During the night the troglodyte had wormed over to the fire. The stretch of rope that ran down his back and knotted his hands to his feet was sooty black. The coals had singed the hair on the creature's backside, but had failed to loose the resourceful fellow from his flaxen bonds. Noting the cave dweller's resonant snore, the man in black quietly lifted himself to his feet, stepped cautiously to the poor creature's side, and with a quick flip of the wrist slipped a choker chain over the troglodyte's head. The brute instantly came to life, gnashing at the man with his teeth. Dar'ock hauled on the chain. The wild man's mouth dropped open and his eyes bulged half out of his head. Dar'ock let the leash go slack. Growling fiercely, and snapping air, the wild man thrashed about on the floor.

"Easy, old boy!" Dar'ock pulled the leash tight again, causing the wild man's face to turn red. "If you don't cooperate I just might be forced to break your neck."

The troglodyte gurgled and coughed. Dar'ock loosed the restraint.

"Chain hurt Garfe!" wailed the cave dweller.

"Ah, so you do have a name!" Dar'ock trumpeted with mock delight. "Well, Garfe, I tell you what, if you will promise to be a good churl I will cut your feet loose, so that you can be my guide dog. And once you have led me to the lair of the enchantress I'll set you free as payment for your services. How does that sound?"

Garfe grunted angrily and sputtered, "I son of Cain!"

Dar'ock wrenched on the chain, and held it firm. "You're a dog, Garfe! Do you understand?" Garfe gagged, and his face looked ready to explode. Dar'ock slackened the leash.

The wild man sucked air. "Garfe a dog! Garfe what-ever you want to call him!" he gasped.

"That's better, Garfe. And I tell you what, as long as you're a good dog you'll suffer no harm, but cross me and you'll find me a very cruel taskmaster."

Dar'ock untied Garfe's feet, but not his hands. He helped the wild man to a sitting position, while keeping tension on the choker chain as a reminder.

Dar'ock picked up his saddle. "Well, Ebony, we've captured ourselves a mountain dog. Could smell the foul thing when we made camp last night. I'm tempted to give it a bath." He swung the saddle onto the horse's back, dropped Garfe's chain, put his foot on it, and proceeded to cinch the girth strap. But as Dar'ock drew up on the cincture, the troglodyte attacked. Sturdy teeth snapped at Dar'ock's ear, but got only the cowl of his heavy coat. Dar'ock could both feel and smell the cave dweller's foul breath. He shuddered with disgust as he cast the stinking creature to the ground, and swift as a cat came down astride its chest. Steel flashed, and a pitiful howl split the cold morning air. Blood dripped from the edge of the man's dagger. He stepped away, scrounged about in his saddlebag, knelt down, and slapped yellow salve on the side of the wild man's head. The troglodyte's shriek nearly shook the mountain. Dar'ock cracked a half smile. "Called gambogen, and applied to raw flesh it stings like a thousand bees. But I presume you'd prefer a little pain to bleeding to death."

Garfe let out a savage, guttural growl. The man in black fired back a menacing glare, reached down with the point of his knife and picked up the wild man's ear from the cavern floor, and held the bloody thing before the pathetic creature's saucer-wide eyes. "You only have two of these,

Garfe." Dar'ock carelessly tossed the wrinkled piece of flesh off to the side. "If you want to lose your other ear, you can try something stupid again just any time."

"Garfe mad!" the wild man snarled.

"Can't say as I blame you." Dar'ock finished cinching Ebony's saddle. "And frankly, Garfe, I would have been angry at you if you had bitten my ear off, as was your intent. In fact, I'd have been angry enough to kill you."

Garfe grunted nonsense in response, and with moiling eyes followed Dar'ock's every move. But he held his rage in check.

With the fire out, and Ebony saddled, Dar'ock mounted up.

"So, lead me to the enchantress' lair, one-eared dog!" The man's ridicule earned another growl, but with shoulders drooping the subdued brute plodded out into the snow. Dar'ock secured the choker chain to his saddle horn and followed.

The wind had spent its energy during the night. Now giant snowflakes floated downward on a docile breeze to take their place as part of the mountain's great white blanket. Dar'ock looked up at the sky. The flakes appeared to fall in slow motion, and a shadow passed through their midst. Dar'ock scowled, wrapped himself in the warmth of his black coat, touched his heels to Ebony's sides, and dogged the troglodyte along the narrow ledge in silence.

Although obedient, the cave dweller groaned and grumbled as he trudged through the deep snow. Dar'ock made sure the feral creature could feel the tightness of the chain.

That day, in spite of a tedious pace, they reached the summit pass, where the wind howled as if angry with their presence. Dar'ock watched as the troglodyte trudged through the cold drifts, and marveled that the creature didn't seem to mind that he was clothed only with his own thick hair, hair that seemed to shed the swirling, wet snow at that. Dar'ock shuddered. Even wrapped in his thick coat he could feel the bite of the cold air that funneled through the pass. Still, they trekked onward, down the other side. Then as night reached out to take the mountain in its grasp, Dar'ock pulled Garfe to a halt and made camp under a large ice laden slab of rock that had broken off the high wall and landed one end on the ledge and the other leaning back against the cliff. The wild man chafed as the man in black tied his feet once again.

"Unfair! Garfe son of Cain. Garfe good guide dog. Dar'ock not kind to Garfe."

Dar'ock laughed, saw to his horse's needs, dressed Garfe's wound, and tossed some jerky and hard bread down by the troglodyte's face. The man in black sneered at the cave dweller and went on about making camp.

Chapter 2
Whisperings of a Soul

Cain knew his wife, and she bore Enoch. And Enoch begot Irad, who begot Mehujael, who begot Methushael, who be-got Lamech, who begot Jabal and Jubal. And Jubal was the father of those who play the flute. The Book of Beginnings

Garfe ate his meal as best he could. He watched the man wrapped in black take out his shiny pipe and put it to his lips. As darkness enveloped their camp it was greeted by a sad aria. The strain ended as discordantly as it had begun. Garfe could not see the man in black, but he imagined him putting away the pipe and nodding off to sleep. The cave dweller growled beneath his breath, squirmed about until he found the most comfortable position possible, which was still anything but comfortable, and tried to sleep.

The next morning they left the shelter of the rock and pushed on through the knee deep snow. About midday, as they neared the base of the high wall, Garfe turned off the main trail that stretched down from the barren heights to the tree laden foothills of the eastern reaches. He took a little used pathway, a narrow ledge that cut across the face of the escarpment around to the north. Neither man saw the shadow that went before them. But they were aware of loose rocks under the thick layer of snow that covered the ledge, and of hanging masses of ice that blocked their way. Dar'ock untied the cave dweller's hands and set him to work removing the mounds of ice from the trail. Garfe grumbled and complained, but he was strong, a hard worker, and the cold didn't seem to bother him.

More than once while Garfe worked at tearing icicles away from the high wall he thought about pouncing on Dar'ock, ripping the leash from his hand, and toppling man and horse over the edge. But he would reach up, tug at his remaining ear, and shake his head no.

In the early afternoon, just after Garfe had broken and cast aside a series of thin ice columns that had barred their way, the mountain began to rumble. He saw Dar'ock look up, followed his gaze, only to see the mountainside collapsing toward them.

"Avalanche! Back, Ebony! Back!" shouted the man in black.

Snow, ice and rocks came crashing down. Garfe saw Dar'ock hauling at Ebony's reins, so he put his shoulder to the stallion's chest and pushed for all he was worth. Masses of snow smashed down on them. Ebony faltered. Dar'ock held him fast. Garfe clung to the horse's neck. The snow inundated them, and nearly tore them from their perch. Pieces of mountain bounced over their heads, slabs of ice skidded by, followed by a large scab of rock that crashed onto the narrow ledge in front of them, splattering snow and ice everywhere. Silence. The avalanche had passed. Dar'ock and Garfe shook off the snow, looked where they had been standing, and together breathed a sigh of relief.

"You know, Garfe, you're not the only one who doesn't want me to find the god. But I won't be stopped." Dar'ock nodded toward the obstruction. "So let's get on with it. Looks top heavy. You shouldn't have any trouble pushing it over the edge. Just be careful you don't go with it."

"Garfe no want to die hanging from chain." The cave dweller glared at Dar'ock, who had maintained his grip on Garfe's leash throughout the whole ordeal.

"Don't worry, wild man, I won't let you hang. If you fall over the edge I'll grant you your freedom. And hey, as far as it is down to the canyon floor, I bet you could have the choker off your neck before you hit bottom. What do you think?"

Garfe snarled, put his back to the high wall, his feet against the massive stone, and shoved it over the edge. He watched the rock fall. He cast Dar'ock a wary eye and mused to himself, "Man in black fast as falling rock. Garfe no fool! But man in black will pay! Yes, he will pay!" He chuckled gruffly and turned back to the trail.

Late in the day they left the snow behind and dropped down into a narrow, boulder-strewn ravine. Garfe was glad Dar'ock decided to call it a day while it was still light out. They had come to a cave formed by huge boulders that looked like two wrestlers on their knees with their arms wrapped around each other's neck, and Dar'ock had commented that they had better take advantage of shelter while it was available. So Garfe found himself once again tied hand and foot while his master went off to scrounge wood for a fire. A bit later he watched Dar'ock return with a handful of sticks, make a fire pit, carve off some shavings, and strike a flame. But how the sticks got in the canyon was a mystery to Garfe. He hadn't seen a tree anywhere.

"What are you putting in fire pan?" Garfe wrinkled his brow, and stared as Dar'ock dumped the contents of a small cloth bag in his pan.

"You'll see, wild man."

A misty smoke rose from the fire pan, and a strange smell filled the air. Garfe wrinkled his nose. He wasn't quite sure if he liked the smell or not. However, the more he sniffed the air, the more the smell appealed to him. He watched in wonder as Dar'ock scooped something from the pan and put it in his mouth.

"You eat stuff burned in fire pan?"

"It's called soup. Here." He took a gourd bowl from his pack and filled it with the steamy stuff. He held up a shaped piece of metal. "You use one of these dippers to get it from the bowl to your mouth, like this."

Garfe shook his head in disgust as he watched the man take another scoop from the fire pan. "Garfe eats raw food. Sometimes warm. Sometimes not warm. No need fire pan."

"Well, tonight you eat my soup or you don't eat at all."

The troglodyte shoulders sagged. "Garfe eat soup stuff from fire pan. It smell good. Garfe hungry."

"All the work you did today, you oughta be hungry." Dar'ock knelt beside Garfe and untied his hands, but much to the cave dweller's dismay the man left his feet tied and the choker chain around his neck.

"Garfe not have to lick food off ground?"

"Nope. Hard to do with soup, besides, I've decided to civilize you, Garfe. How do you like that?"

"Garfe son of Cain!"

Dar'ock laughed and handed Garfe a steaming bowl and a dipper. Garfe willingly received the food, and immediately set to slurping it down. When he was finished he wiped his mouth on his hairy arm, and let out a satisfied grunt. "Good stuff."

"What's your usual fare?" Dar'ock set aside the fire pan, leaned against a rock, and picked at his teeth while he waited for the wild man's answer.

Garfe made one final, obnoxious slurp as he ran his tongue over the bottom of the bowl. He wiped his arm across his mouth again, and pressed a hand against his belly. He let out a belch and sighed.

Dar'ock tilted his head to one side, and the corners of his mouth curled downward. "So, back to my question, Garfe, what do you usually eat?"

The cave dweller's eyes scanned the floor and walls of the shelter. "Garfe munch furry-crawly things, bird's eggs, cave spiders, rock beetles. If it moves Garfe eats it." He walked a hairy hand over the ground imitating a bug seeking cover, and cocked a hopeful eyebrow at his captor. "Garfe catch Dar'ock crunchy, juicy bug?"

Dar'ock waved a hand in front of his face, and grimaced in disgust. "No thank you, Garfe. We civilized Sons of Cain don't eat rock beetles, or any such creepy things."

In response the troglodyte growled, "Humph! Garfe son of Cain. Garfe know what's good. Garfe like tasty beetles."

Dar'ock rose to his feet and picked up the cord he used to bind Garfe's hands. The hair on the back of the cave dweller's neck bristled. A growl rolled in his throat. Steel flashed, and he found himself staring at Dar'ock's dagger. "Garfe good guide dog!" he whimpered. And without further resistance he let Dar'ock tie his hands to his feet.

Dar'ock suddenly stood up and looked toward the entrance to the cave. His brow furrowed, and his jaw went tight. "Again it passes by?"

"What Dar'ock see?"

"See? Humph! It isn't visible to the eye, but still its presence is as real as yours or mine. It opposes me...but I will not be stayed!"

Garfe had no idea what the man might be talking about. Still, the very idea of some unseen danger, and him lying there tied up like a rat in a snare, struck fear to his heart. But the man in black showed no outward signs of apprehension.

Dar'ock sauntered to the opposite side of the shelter, eased himself down to the hard, cold floor, enfolded himself in his black coat, and pulled out his flute.

"Why make awful noise with shiny pipe?" Garfe wished he could plug his ear. He didn't like Dar'ock's doleful tunes.

Dar'ock sighed and looked off into nothingness. "My playing gives voice to my soul, and it is the whispering of my soul that has set me on this quest."

"Quest?" Garfe had difficulty even pronouncing the word.

"Quest. You know, to go in search of something." Dar'ock put the pipe to his lips, and Garfe groaned. The man in black played for a while, slipped the pipe back inside his coat and hunkered down and went to sleep.

Garfe wormed this way and that, and eventually fell into a restless slumber. It was the middle of the night when his eyes suddenly popped open. The cave dweller trembled, but not from the cold. A scent hung on the air, a scent that turned his blood to ice. Garfe found himself wanting to call out to Dar'ock, to warn the man in black, but he dared not. After all, a fangcat could hear a pine needle drop on a rocky ledge! In his mind's eye Garfe saw the huge cat with its brown furry coat, blazing yellow eyes and long, curved fangs. He craned his neck to search the shadows of the moonlit canyon beyond the small grotto. He could see little to nothing, but he sensed the creature drawing closer. Garfe's panic grew. He looked to where his master lay sleeping. The man in black was gone!

The horse let out a ghastly whinny, and its hooves clattered on the stone floor. Garfe's heart hammered at his chest. He strained at the ropes that bound his hands and feet. Then he felt it, the creature's presence. Not out in the canyon. He felt it near. Terror flayed his emotions. He pivoted his gaze, and what he had seen in his mind became reality. The massive fangcat stood in the opening to the cave, its eyes lusting for flesh, its dagger-like teeth bared, and its muscles tensed, ready to pounce and sink its teeth into Garfe's quaking carcass! He couldn't help himself, Garfe screamed the man in black's name. "Dar'ooock!"

The cat hesitated. A shadow fell from the darkness above. The light of the moon betrayed a flash of steel. The fangcat's eyes glazed. Blood gushed from its mouth. The shadow leapt away. Garfe watched the huge cat convulse. Once. Twice. And then it fell dead, not five feet from Garfe's face. The cave dweller shuddered as he watched the creature's life pool about its head. And Garfe's eyes, moiling with anger and awe, sheered from the cat to look up at the man in black.

Dar'ock stepped forward and nudged the cat with his foot. "Big fella', isn't he? Easily eight feet rump to nose. Must weigh nearly as much as Ebony." He shook his head, turned to Garfe. "How you doing, wild man?"

"Garfe not wild man! Garfe son of Cain. Him not afraid of fangcat."

Dar'ock roared with laughter. "Nooo, Garfe not afraid of fangcat. Not after I cut its throat. But that scream, Garfe. Absolute terror! Nooo, wild man not afraid!"

"Garfe helpless. Garfe tied up by mean Dar'ock."

"Yes, but if Dar'ock didn't bind Garfe with strong cords, Dar'ock would get no sleep. But Dar'ock took good care of you, Garfe. After all, he didn't let the fang-cat eat you for breakfast, did he?"

Garfe held his tongue. He didn't want to admit that what Dar'ock said was true. He did not want to admit that he felt gratitude toward his captor.

Chapter 3
Valley of No Return

The Lord said to Cain, "Why are you angry?" Cain rose up against Abel his brother and killed him. And the Lord said, "The voice of spilled blood cries to me from the ground. So now you are cursed." And the Lord marked Cain. The Book of Beginnings

Dar'ock slipped the choker chain around Garfe's neck, untied his feet, paused and gave Garfe a cautioning look before untying his hands.

"Where do we go from here, Garfe?"

Garfe grunted something indistinguishable and pointed toward a nebulous place off in the distance. Dar'ock smirked, swung into the saddle, and gestured for Garfe to take the lead.

"Why you want me take you to enchantress?" Garfe asked the question as he turned his feet to the narrow trail that split the canyon.

"Well wild man, I'm searching for the god. In the land of Nod there are those who claim that the enchantress is a goddess. The old ones have vast knowledge, and they say she is a human offspring brought forth by a divine being. So, I'm presuming she will be able to tell me where I can find the god."

Garfe glowered over his shoulder at Dar'ock. He cocked a bushy eyebrow, and waved a large hand in the air. "If Deva is daughter of the god then the god is not good. Dar'ock not smart looking for the god."

Dar'ock grinned broadly and leaned forward on his saddle horn. "Well, Garfe, when I meet this Deva woman, perhaps I should let her know what you think of her?"

Garfe beetled his bushy eyebrows into a scowl, and turned back to the path, padding on in peevish silence.

Dar'ock ignored the cave dweller's foul mood, and continued chattering on about his quest. "It is said that the god lay with Dedra, Cain's eldest daughter. Dedra was a base woman, not much better than you troglodytes. So, as a result of the union, Deva has the vileness of her mother mingled with the puissant nature of the god. Do you know what the word puissant means, wild man? It means powerful. Deva is evil and power personified. And yes, I admit, that's a strange mix. But anyway, I'm confident she can tell me where I can find the god."

"The god curse the sons of Cain. Garfe not want to find the god."

"Yes, that is the issue, isn't it, Garfe. And cursed though we are, we seem to have everything but peace. So, we will find the god, and have words with him, Garfe."

"Garfe not have words with the god. Garfe want nothing to do with the god!"

"Yes sir, Garfe, you're not afraid of anything or anybody...except fangcats and the god!" Dar'ock laughed tauntingly.

Garfe shrugged his burly shoulders and hissed curses under his breath.

The man in black ignored the cave dweller's mutterings. He would allow the churl that much. But like it or not, Garfe was going to help him find the god, or at least find out where to look for the god.

After they had tracked another mile or so, Dar'ock gave the cave dweller's tether a slight tug to get his attention. "So, Garfe, how far is it to the enchantress' lair?"

"Not far." And although Dar'ock pressed for more, that was all the answer he got.

A day later the unlikely traveling companions left the narrow canyon, and trekked across a desolate, scree-scattered valley toward a gap in the far palisade.

As he led the man in black along the stony trail, Garfe worked on his thoughts. No, he would not tell Dar'ock that Deva lived in the Valley of No Return. Nor would he tell him that others had passed through the gate, and never been seen again. Garfe knew, because Garfe's people were the watchers. They guarded the Way to the dread valley. Dread, because the enchantress required a yearly sacrifice, a child under ten years of age.

Garfe remembered the last time he visited the watchers. He could still see the face of the blond haired girl-child they had sent to the enchantress' altar. A pretty face sheeted with fear. And she had smiled at him.

The troglodyte's mouth spilled to a frown. He trekked along, stoop shouldered, anger creasing his brow. He had sorrowed for the child that had been stolen from a distant village, but if not her, one of the watcher's own children would have to have been sacrificed. And had not the nephilim, who carried the child off to the Valley of No Return, told him and the others how the children were bound hand and foot, laid on a great stone altar, and... Garfe thrust the thought aside with a shudder. He closed his eyes seeking to escape the terror, but saw the giant's bearded face, heard his coarse laughter, and the awful echo of the little girl's fearful cries as she was carried off into the darkness.

"That why Garfe never mate!" he mumbled to himself.

He screwed his neck around and eyeballed the man in black. He sighed and quickly turned away, relieved that the man was looking out over the valley, and showed no interest in his mutterings. "Humph!" grunted the troglodyte. "Man in black not care about the children. Garfe no brute. Garfe son of Cain. Garfe feel pain for children."

The troglodyte's languid face twitched. The corners of his cheeks lifted. A slight glint broke the dullness of his eyes. "This time I will not be sending child to the enchantress." Nerves on edge, he breathed the words inaudibly with furtive looks back at the man in black.

Late morning brought the travelers to the break in the high wall. They passed through a long, narrow rift and came out into an expansive gorge scattered with large boulders, and enclosed round about by vertical bulwarks of solid granite.

Once again an unseen shadow crossed their path. Dar'ock stiffened. He could feel the malevolence of the spirit being. Dar'ock's lip curled into a snarl. But the shade was the least of his problems. The troglodyte was his main concern. The creature's mood seemed to grow fouler with every step. "Garfe, you wouldn't play false with me, would you?" Dar'ock's eyes searched the canyon surveying every inch of ground, and every place of shadow. The hair on the nape of his neck stood on end, and hot ice shot up his spine. "If this is a trap, you'll die choking on your own blood, Garfe."

"Garfe good guide dog!" whimpered the troglodyte. He gave Dar'ock a pitiful look that dripped with disappointment, but his performance did not hide his contempt. "Dar'ock not need to worry. Garfe take him to enchantress. Garfe not play games."

"Well, wild man, this is a box canyon if ever I've seen one. The wall there at the far end must be three hundred feet high." Accusation edged Dar'ock's voice.

"See, Dar'ock not trust Garfe." The cave dweller pulled his eyebrows down into a scowl, and folded his arms across his chest. "If Dar'ock not trust Garfe, Garfe not take to enchantress. Dar'ock can go find enchantress by himself."

Dar'ock sniggered and shot another quick glance around the walled-in gorge. "Well, if that's your ploy, then I have no choice but to trust you! Anyway, Garfe, what good would you be dead, or minus two ears? Either way you'd become carrion for a fangcat. So onward, wild man."

Garfe growled and sputtered, but pressed forward. Dar'ock grinned. His grip tightened on the choker chain. Other troglodytes were out there. The stench of their fetid bodies grew stronger. "The scheming wretch!" Dar'ock mused to himself. And while his mind perused the possibilities of what Garfe might be up to, his eyes scanned the shadows. Nothing moved.

By mid-afternoon the primary source of the rancid odor had fallen behind, and the canyon wall stood yet unbroken in front of them. Dar'ock's free hand rested on the hilt of the broadsword strapped to his saddle. He directed Ebony with his knees, and his eyes attended every penumbra cast by every column of rock.

"Garfe, if your friends attack, you'll not just lose your good ear. With a wrench of this chain I'll sever your head from your body!" Dar'ock hissed the words just loud enough for the cave dweller alone to hear.

Garfe stopped and glared over his shoulder. Deep ruts etched his brow. "My people the watchers of gate. They not attack Dar'ock. Garfe not dumb. We have come to the Way. Deva's lair other side of canyon wall."

"And just how do we get to the other side of the wall?" Dar'ock's voice leached sarcasm as he gestured with his eyebrows toward the sheer cliff that blocked the way.

"Garfe not go other side of wall." The cave dweller's scowl deepened. "Garfe not pass gate. Dar'ock go to Deva's lair by himself."

"If there's a hole in the wall, you're leading me through it, Garfe." Threat edged Dar'ock's growl, but Garfe stood his ground, arms crossed, and eyes ablaze.

"Move it, wild man!"

The command went unheeded.

"You slow pated troglodyte! Why are you just standing there? Get on with it!"

"Dar'ock go alone." Garfe set his jaw, and looked away. "Garfe not pass through the Way. Not even for mean master."

"You will pass through the hole, Garfe, because I demand that you lead me to the very door of the enchantress' lair!" Dar'ock jerked on Garfe's tether. "You're my guide dog, remember?"

The cave dweller's fingers worked at the chain. He gasped for air. But not until his hands went limp did Dar'ock let the choker go slack. Garfe's knees wobbled, he sucked air, but he remained fixed in place.

"Garfe go no farther!" rasped the cave dweller. He motioned toward the wall. "Enchantress lives in valley beyond gate. Garfe lead you to enchantress, now Dar'ock let Garfe go free."

Dar'ock propped himself on his saddle horn, and glared down at the troglodyte. He felt like giving the chain a jerk that would pop the wretched creature's head free from its foul body, but with effort he refrained himself.

"So where's the gate, Garfe? All I see is rock wall and boulders."

"Dar'ock still not trust Garfe."

The cave dweller pivoted on his heels. Dar'ock followed him past one of the huge boulders at the base of the escarpment. The sparkle returned to Dar'ock's eyes when he saw the eight-foot by eight-foot black hole in the face of the cliff. He dismounted and turned to the cave dweller. "Garfe, if you prove false in this matter I'll hunt you down, and... Well, you know what I'm capable of, wild man."

"Garfe, he not false! Garfe good guide dog. Dar'ock go through gate and follow the Way to where enchantress live."

Dar'ock frowned, stepped over to Garfe and removed the chain from around his neck. "You've served me well, Garfe. And, hey, sorry about the ear." Dar'ock laid his hand on Garfe's shoulder as a gesture of goodwill. Instantly Garfe's teeth flashed. The cave dweller bit down on Dar'ock's forearm. The man in black wrenched his arm free, and Garfe was off, his wide, leathery feet slapping the rock floor of the canyon as he went.

The troglodyte's cuspids ripped coat, not flesh. Dar'ock gripped his bruised arm, and watched Garfe scurry off to join his friends behind a distant boulder. The cave dweller's laughter echoed off the canyon walls. And in spite of the pain, Dar'ock laughed with him.

"I take it you enjoyed your taste of revenge, Garfe! I tell you what, wait for me here, and when I return I'll let you know how things went with the enchantress!" The man in black's call echoed off distant canyon walls. Then with the corner of his mouth twisted into a grin, he turned away from the watchers and led Ebony to the black hole that breached the high wall.

Dar'ock approached the gate, took one last look over his shoulder and entered the Way. He stopped. The corner of his mouth fell. He could feel the presence of the haunting spirit more strongly than ever before. Had he actually seen the spirit's shadow pass by? Ebony skittered nervously. Dar'ock stroked the stallion's muzzle, and whispered settling words. He set his jaw and continued on.

"Hmm. Not what I expected, Ebony. Looked like a black hole, but it's well lit."

About thirty paces inside the dark opening a torch protruded from the smooth rock wall. And every fifteen cubits or so another cresset lit the way. "Interesting place, Ebony. Looks like Garfe may have actually pointed us in the right direction."

Dar'ock approached, and carefully examined, one of the torches. His eyes widened and his brow rose. "How do you like that, Ebony? It burns without pitch. Appears to be some kind of perpetual flame." He reached in his saddlebag, and after some searching pulled out a glove. He slipped it on his hand, reached up, and snuffed out the flame. He pulled Ebony in closer, stuck his foot in a stirrup, lifted himself by the saddle horn, and looked in the bowl of the strange lamp.

"Hollow. That's odd." Although the flame was no longer present, something cool effused from the pole of the torch. Dar'ock pulled away, shook his head, dropped back to the ground, and led Ebony deeper into the mountain. His face drew into a grimace. He could still feel the presence of the shadow that had passed. Did he hear mocking laughter? Or was it the caw of a raven?

He passed one torch. Two. Three. BOOM! The tunnel turned into a ball of flame. The blast singed Dar'ock's coat and sent him sprawling. Ebony's reins slipped from his hand, and with nostrils flaring, and eyes wide with terror, the stallion bolted. For a moment Dar'ock heard the clatter of hooves. But when he looked up, Ebony was gone. Dar'ock rolled to his side and turned his gaze back to where the blast had originated. A blue flame danced on the now misshapen head of the torch he had smothered. "Well, you didn't have to get violent!" He huffed, but laughter edged his voice. He lifted himself from the hard stone floor, dusted off, and followed after Ebony.

By the time Dar'ock reached the other end of the tunnel, the sun had dipped behind a distant escarpment, and nightshade was beginning to cast its gray spell. Some thirty strides off to the left he spotted Ebony grazing near a stand of willen trees. Beyond the trees a grassy meadow eased down toward the floor of a broad dale.

"A fertile valley nestled in a great canyon. After all the high country desolation it seems out of place." Dar'ock let his eyes scan the rock wall that apparently encircled the lush basin. His gaze shifted to the forest in the middle of the valley where a curious fortress with numerous tower-like spires rose above the trees.

"Well, Garfe, it seems you did keep your end of the bargain." He pushed the cowl back off his head, smiled, and rubbed his forearm. "And you got in the last lick besides."

Dar'ock drifted over to Ebony. "Well, fella, where shall we spend the night? Think you can handle the shade of a willen tree, rather than the dark recesses of a mountain cave?" He took the stallion's reins and led him under the spreading branches of the nearest tree, tethered him with freedom to graze, and made camp for the night. After a cold meal he settled back against the trunk of the rough barked willen tree, pulled out his silver pipe, and shrilled a song that seemed to mourn the dying of the day. With a sigh, he put away the flute, rolled himself in his black coat, and let his eyelids sag shut.

And so night came, and a pitchy darkness engulfed the dale. But the alabaster orb that rules the night wrestled with the swarthy gloom, and the result was a shroud of enchantment. And with the magic cast by the moon came a striking figure dressed in a red coursing robe, gliding silently through the shadows toward the man in black.

The woman hesitated, looked down at the motionless trespasser, her smile sardonic. She slipped over to where Ebony pulled at his tether. Whispering gentle words, the woman reached out and stroked the wary stallion's neck, gained his confidence, and led him from beneath the tree. With an easy grace she swung up astraddle his back. Ebony skittered a bit, but otherwise did not resist. Dar'ock watched through squinted eyes as the woman quietly rode down the slope toward the haze-swathed fortress. And a shadow that had the look of a raven spread its wings and followed.

"I thought as much. Tis' the shadow of death itself that has been nipping at my heels! But alas, now it has turned aside to imperil another poor soul!" The corner of Dar'ock's mouth twitched into a smirk. He pulled his cloak in tight, closed his eyes, and finished the night.

Chapter 4
The Enchantress

When men began to multiply on the face of the earth, the sons of the God saw the daughters of men and took wives for themselves.   The Book of Beginnings

The dawn chased away the shades that haunted the night, and Dar'ock tossed Ebony's saddle over his shoulder and headed down into the vale. The distance to the enchantress' fortress proved greater than he had reckoned. The sun stood almost straight overhead when he arrived at the gate. As he contemplated how to announce his arrival, gears began to squeak and grind, and the mesh grating that blocked his way lifted, allowing him entrance. He proceeded with caution, but as he cleared the inner edge of the wall he heard the portcullis slam shut behind him. Instinctively he glanced back over his shoulder. A cloud of dust obscured the iron gate.

"So, she has sprung her trap. Humph! If she thinks she has caught her prey, she can think again!" Dar'ock turned, and let his gaze sweep the exquisitely groomed courtyard that stretched up to the fortress keep. A little girl, who looked to Dar'ock to be about twelve years old, loped across the green in his direction, shimmering blond tresses streaming behind her. The sight of the seemingly carefree youngster brought a smile to Dar'ock's face. He eased Ebony's saddle from his shoulder to the ground.

"Hello." The girl's voice rang with cheerfulness, and her sky blue eyes sparkled with life. "I'm Yennea. Welcome to Wonderland."

"I'm Dar'ock." Dar'ock shifted his eyes from the joyful girl to the drab looking keep. "This place doesn't look much like a wonderland."

"Wonderland is what I call it."

Dar'ock turned his gaze back to Yennea and studied her face. *The poor creature is oblivious to her harsh surroundings and the pall that hangs on the air,* he mused to himself, and then he voiced his thought as a question. "And why do you call this hideaway Wonder-land?"

Yennea lilted her head to one side and laughed airily. "Because I wonder why it's always summer here. I wonder how someone as knowing as the queen can be so cruel. I wonder how she can look so beautiful one moment, and so...well, different the next. I wonder why I am not allowed to walk in the woods outside the great wall. And sometimes I wonder why I am here, and how I got here. I remember bits and pieces, but the images are not clear."

Dar'ock quirked the corner of his mouth, and nodded. "Well then, I guess this is Wonderland, isn't it. And I must admit, I wonder about a few things too."

"And what do you wonder about?" Yennea's eyes sparkled like sunshine on water in anticipation of Dar'ock's answer.

"Well, first I wonder this," Dar'ock reached down and let his hand brush the edge of the girl's silky locks, "Where did you get such pretty yellow hair? I have never seen a daughter of Cain with yellow hair."

"Oh, I'm not a daughter of Cain." Yennea cocked an eyebrow, and a distant look passed across her face. "I am a Daughter of Seth, from the Plain of Jared. My mother's name is Nadena and my father's is Lamech, but I don't remember much from those days."

The girl's revelation pleased Dar'ock. He had heard of the children of Seth but had never actually seen one of them. He let his eyes take in all her features. She not only had yellow hair and blue eyes, but also a thin face with fine lines, and a small but maturing frame. *The daughters of Seth are desirable. But this one is just a child. Still...* He pulled his eyes away, and cast aside his lewd thoughts. "Well, daughter of Seth, I wonder how old you were when you came here?"

Yennea smiled broadly. "I was seven when I was taken from my parents by the hairy beast men. They gave me to the hunter, who brought me here."

"And how long have you been here?"

"Six years."

Dar'ock grimaced. "Six years in the lair of the enchantress?"

Yennea's face wrinkled into questions. "The what?"

"Just big words that describe this fortress." He motioned with his hand from the wall toward the keep while studying her face. "Are you happy here, Yennea?"

The girl laughed. "I'm happy anywhere! Aren't you happy wherever you are?"

Dar'ock's mouth crimped to a frown. "No. Not really. I laugh a lot. But happy?" He slowly shook his head and stared off into space.

"I don't understand." Yennea wrinkled her nose. "How can you smile and laugh and not be happy?"

Dar'ock muttered something about life being cruel, and that only the heartless survive. Yennea answered with a blank stare.

"Anyway, Yennea, I'm glad you're happy." Dar'ock wondered at his own words. He had never in his life cared whether or not someone else was happy. He shook it off. "Yennea, you spoke of a queen. I presume her name is Deva. I have come seeking an audience with her. So that is something else that I wonder. Would you be so kind as to take me to her?"

Yennea's face became animated with remembrance. "Oh, yes!" she chirped. "In fact, that is the very thing the queen sent me to do."

Yennea took Dar'ock by the hand. He picked up his saddle, and accompanied her across the lawn toward the keep. Dar'ock glanced about at the empty courtyard. From somewhere a raven scolded their passing. Dar'ock thought it strange that he had not seen anyone, other than the girl, since he stepped through the gate. "Yennea, there is something else I wonder about."

"Yes?"

"Does anyone else live here?"

"You wonder many things, just like me." Yennea looked up at the man in black, giggled, and waved a hand. "Of course there are others who live here. The cook. The maid. The grounds keeper. And, of course, the hunter, and also the dungeon keeper. None of them ever speak to me, so I don't know any of their names. Oh yes, and sometimes I hear sad voices rising from below. The sound is like that of weeping children. My mistress told me the sad voices are the souls of the dead." Yennea looked up into Dar'ock's face. A deep sorrow filled her eyes. "I'm not happy when I hear the sad voices. They cry in the night, and I cry with them."

Dar'ock marveled at her revelation. They entered the keep, so he didn't pursue the subject any further. He set Ebony's saddle off to the side. "I'll tend to this later."

Yennea led him along what appeared to be the main hall. The walls inside the keep were as plain as the outer walls. No pictures or cloth hangings, just cobwebs and dust. Even the marble floor needed cleaning. But then, if there was only one maid to care for the place she would surely not be able to keep up with everything!

They came to a large, ornate wooden door. Yennea shouldered it open, and tension exploded outward riding the air on angry words.

"You stupid little wench!" The enchantress' voice rang out high pitched and screechy as she hissed a line of expletives at the young girl.

The enchantress stood on a dais, hands gripped white-knuckled at her sides, her face livid with rage. "I told you to bring the visitor to me immediately. But no, you stand around and chatter the time away. Well, time is mine, you dawdling little fool! So clamp your jabbering jaws, and do as you're told! Now, off to your place, miserable waif!"

At the enchantress' outburst, Dar'ock's eyes blazed with anger. He grated his teeth, and glanced down at Yennea. He was amazed to find that in spite of the queen's harsh words the girl's smile remained.

When the queen finished her tirade, Yennea bowed politely, turned and hurriedly walked over to a stool in the far corner of the chamber.

Dar'ock watched the girl cross the room. He shook his head. "That girl is a very young thirteen, but someday she will be a very beautiful woman." But he held the thought only briefly. The enchantress' frothy voice demanded his attention.

"I only keep the little tart because of her pretty yellow curls."

Dar'ock shifted his gaze from Yennea to the queen's dais. Her lavish throne, ornately sculpted and overlaid with gold, was one with the pyramid-like block on which it sat. The raven having become more material than shadow, watched from the back of the throne. A veil that exuded an aromatic mist encircled the dais. The ethereal curtain was broken by a red swathed walkway that extended up the six steps ending at the base of the throne. Dar'ock scowled in puzzlement, for although the room reeked of incense, he had not noticed the sweet odor when he first entered. In fact, his first impression was that the chamber smelled a bit musty, but perhaps it was just the hallway that had smelled musty. The man in black stepped to the opening in the mist barrier and lifted his gaze to the enchantress.

The old sage who had told Dar'ock about the enchantress had warned him not to look in her eyes. But Dar'ock prided himself in not being superstitious. The woman's charms did not worry him. And so he sought her eyes, livid black pupils set against a background of lucent yellow. There was no white, and strangely, she seemed to have no eyelids. "Eyes like a serpent!" The thought startled Dar'ock. He took a step backward, but Deva held his gaze. She offered a disarming smile, and instantly his concerns melted away. And although his eyes were locked with hers, he was aware of her tongue gently caressing the edge of her full, and perfectly formed lips, and of skin, soft, smooth, and touchable. And it confused him that he had not previously noticed that her floor length auburn hair covered her unclothed body like a living garment. Dar'ock sucked in a deep breath of pungent air. "Yes, this is Wonderland!" He mused to himself. A caw reminded him of the presence of the Shadow of Death, but he refused to look away from the enchantress.

Deva laughed and her lucent shroud shimmered about her body. Appetite heated Dar'ock's blood. "She is mine for the taking!" And as if hearing his thought, Deva laughed again, a coarse laugh. The direction of Dar'ock's thoughts altered. "But if I take her, she'll not be mine. I'll be hers!" That impression repelled him. He tried to tear his gaze away from the enchantress, but his eyes did not turn aside. Now her delicious laughter tickled his ears. With a fluid-like motion she shifted her weight. Dar'ock's passion intensified, and his doubts fled. "Yes, I shall take her!"

"I've been expecting you, Prince of Nod."

Deva's smooth voice brought to mind the scent of his favorite red wine, and deepened his craving for her. She ran a long, narrow tantalizing finger along the curve of her cheek. In the background, the raven gabbled.

"Thank you for the gift." Deva laughed softly.

"Gift?" An inquisitive expression crossed Dar'ock's face.

"Yes, all who walk the Way of Life must bring a gift." The enchantress' words came like the purring of a cat. "The great stallion you gave me will make a wonderful addition to my stable."

Dar'ock offered no protest. For the moment he chose to humor the woman.

"So, Prince of Nod, tell me, why have you come to the Valley of the Living?"

"I've come here looking for your father."

"My father?" Surprise crossed Deva's face.

"Yes, I would have words with the god."

"With the god?" Mockery edged the question that rolled off her lips. "And you think, good prince, that you'll find him here?"

A broad grin spread Dar'ock's face. "So it is true, you are the daughter of the god? And is it also true that Dedra, Cain's eldest daughter, is your mother?"

The enchantress forced a smile, but her eyes momentarily brandished anger. "Yes, Dedra is my mother. And the god, Lucifer, is my father. He possessed Farank, Cain's great grandson, and Farank bedded my mother, and so I came to be."

"But isn't Farank your mother's demented brother?"

"Not demented. Possessed! There is a difference, you know."

Confusion creased Dar'ock's brow. "The god possessed Farank?"

"Yes, the god, Lucifer, chose to become through Farank." Deva no longer purred, and behind her, the raven squawked testily. The enchantress' words snarled from between tightly pressed lips. "You are of lower intelligence than I thought, Prince of Nod."

"Lucifer is the god?" Dar'ock ignored Deva's peevish outburst.

"Lucifer is greater than the god!" Deva sprang to her feet. The raven fluttered its wings and cawed angrily. Rage flared across the enchantress' face. In that same instant she lost eye contact with Dar'ock. She whirled, and gestured toward Yennea as she did so. "Go Prince of Nod, Yennea will take you to your room. We will continue this conversation at another time." And with that the enchantress slithered around her throne, glided down the dais, through the emanating mist, and into the darkness beyond. The raven shadowed her.

Dar'ock felt Yennea's hand slip into his. After his encounter with the enchantress, the girl's touch stirred emotions. He looked down at her and willfully drove the vile thoughts from his mind. The girl smiled and tugged at his sleeve. He turned and left the queen's chamber.

When they reached the hallway, Dar'ock realized that Yennea was snickering.

"And what do you find so funny, daughter of Seth?"

"Oh, I find it amusing that anyone would come here looking for God. He can be found anywhere, but this seems like an odd place to look for Him."

"What do you know about the god?" Arrogance edged Dar'ock's voice. "You're just a child."

Yennea fell silent. She guided him down the hall to an elegantly provided chamber. As they entered the room, Yennea checked the corridor and hurriedly closed the door. When she turned to face Dar'ock she still displayed her resilient smile. Dar'ock wondered if the girl ever frowned.

"Be careful, Prince of Nod." Yennea glanced toward the door. "Deva does not like to talk about God. She hates God, as does her father, Lucifer. They do all within their power to make God unhappy. But they shall not succeed."

Having a thirteen-year-old girl give him instruction caused Dar'ock to bristle. What's more, with his anger came the desire to throw Yennea on the bed, rip off her clothes, and... She would not be the first young girl he had ravaged! But something stopped him. In spite of the intensity of his lust, he could not bring himself to touch the girl.

"Leave!" He growled. "I can take care of myself. I don't need instruction from a child."

Yennea shook her head. "You come looking for God, but you will not have a child point you to him. How then shall you ever find him?"

"Get out!" Dar'ock jerked open the door, and motioned toward the hall. Yennea curtsied and left the room.

Chapter 5
The Raven's Cackle

Then the Lord saw that man's wickedness was great, and that every intent and thought that came from his heart was only evil. The Book of Beginnings

*E*erie sounds came from the keep and carried out across the vale. A nighthawk swept down from its perch on the high wall, and with the bird of prey came darkness.

Inside the keep shadows moved along the walls of the dimly lit hall. Rusty hinges squeaked. And the enchantress slinked into Dar'ock's bedchamber. Dar'ock looked up. Their eyes met. His passions kindled. The candle on the lamp stand next to the bed flickered and went out. And just as the light died Dar'ock thought he saw a dark shape enter his room behind Deva. Dar'ock laid aside his silver pipe, reached out into the darkness, and took Deva's hand. She resisted, but only briefly. He drew her to him and indulged his lust.

As he lay holding his prize the corner of his mouth twisted into a dark smile. *I said I would have her!* Still, the doing of the deed left him with a hollow feeling in his gut. In fact, for the first time in his life he felt used. And that realization infuriated him. He was the user, never the used! He loosed his grip.

Deva slithered from his bed. "And so, Prince of Nod, you eat of the seeds you have sown." The candle came to life. Deva turned and faced him.

Dar'ock ignored her words. Expecting to further stimulate his lust, he shifted his gaze from the ceiling to the woman he had just bedded. Horror sheered the smug expression from his face. He gaped at dull ashen hair that hung limp over an emaciated carcass of pallid yellow flesh. And from the enchantress' gaunt face death laughed at him. From the back of a nearby chair the raven cackled.

"You...you are wretched! I don't understand." Dar'ock felt agitated with himself for not having noticed her condition when she walked into his chamber. He ran his hand through his hair, and did his best to avoid looking Deva in the eye.

"I am dying."

"But this morning you looked so..."

Deva laughed, but her laughter quickly became a raspy cough. "An illusion, Prince of Nod. You should not have looked into my eyes."

"What makes you think you're dying?" He glanced at her, but immediately wrenched his eyes away. *Loathsome!* His stomach rolled, and he shuddered visibly.

The enchantress frowned pensively. "I have spread my legs for many a man and a few women as well. Now I pay the price. The god has cursed me to die the death. But don't look so appalled, Prince of Nod, for what you see is but a mirror of what you yourself will become."

Deva pivoted on her heels and left the room. The shadow of death followed. Caws of harsh laughter echoed from the hall and died away into the depths of the dismal keep. Dar'ock sat on the edge of his bed staring at the vacant doorway.

Dar'ock wandered listlessly about the palace. No one hindered him, though he did find that some doors were kept locked. Also, he never again saw the enchantress, and had no desire to see her. An aged, prune-faced maid brought his meals. A hunchback gardener worked lazily out in the courtyard. The only other person he saw was Yennea. And as Dar'ock meandered about he struggled with indecision. He had no idea where to go in search of the god. And although he had no reason to stay at the fortress, he felt no compulsion to leave. So each night a discordant melody issued from the keep, then silence.

One day, after seeing to Ebony's needs, Dar'ock once again explored the keep, looking for something that would give some insight as to where he might find the god. In an anteroom he came across an engraved scene from the Garden of Eden, the focal point of which was a smiling serpent hanging from a tree branch. *Yes, Eden!* He turned away with less heaviness in his step.

He left the anteroom and headed down the central hallway. But he had not gone far when he noticed that a door previously locked, now stood ajar. He approached the door, but quickly backed away. Malodorous air vented out into the hall. "The stench of death!" he muttered. He covered his nose and mouth with a piece of cloth and pressed forward. The door opened into a short hallway lit by torches like those he had seen when he passed through the mountain. At the end of the hallway a second door opened to a steep stairway. Dar'ock spiraled down the cobbled stairs and cautiously inched out into an immense circular chamber dimly lit by six of the peculiar wall cressets. A quick look from left to right revealed that the place was deserted. "Little wonder!" He mused inwardly. "No one could stand this fetid smell for long!"

Dar'ock stepped out into the dungeon and encountered a macabre scene. Rusty chains dangled from a damp stone wall, some of the irons still imprisoning small cadavers, while others held but whitened bones. Few of the manacles hung empty. But Dar'ock's eyes quickly moved to the middle of the domed cavern, where he found himself gaping at a huge altar, a pile of smallish bones, and numerous tiny, shrivel skinned carcasses. Dar'ock's stomach unhinged. He ripped his eyes from the horror before him and fled back up the stairs.

Dar'ock burst out into the main hallway gasping for air. He slammed the door behind and momentarily leaned on his knees before going over to one of the alcoves that opened to the outside. There he gulped in fresh air and gazed blurry eyed off into nothingness. Finally, grating his teeth, he wiped his eyes, and turned back to the closed door.

"So that's the source of Yennea's tears!" He shook his head. "I had no idea!"

Chapter 6
The Hunter

And there were mighty giants on the earth in those days, and also afterward, when the sons of the God came in to the daughters of men and bore children to them. The Book of Beginnings

*I*t was later that same day that Dar'ock saw the hunter for the first time. The brute, nearly seven cubits tall, tromped across the courtyard toward the fortress. He carried a huge broadsword at his side, and a longbow slung across his back. But the giant's pitted face, menacing eyes, and mangy, black beard most effected his intimidating aura. The corner of Dar'ock's mouth moldered into a scowl. "Little wonder the watchers fear him. Even I wouldn't want to buck that strapper!"

Night came, and the moon, having passed through its cycle, once again spread the vale with eerie enchantment. Tension seemed to drip from the air like heavy dew. Dar'ock sat in the window ledge of his bedchamber, silver pipe in hand, watching tendrils of mist crawl over the outer wall of the fortress. He draped his arms around his knees, and leaned his head back against the stone casement.

"The Valley of Life." He muttered the words under his breath. His face warped into a frown. "Humph! There is no life here. This is a place of death!"

Dar'ock's thoughts turned to Yennea. She often accompanied him when he wandered about the palace and its grounds. A wry smile crossed his face. "Fact is," he thought, "that girl's the only bit of light in this whole dismal fortress!" He put away his flute, swung his feet to the floor, and paced over to the bed. He flopped down and stared at the ceiling, until his eyes finally drooped shut from weariness. But sleep brought dreadful visitants. Dar'ock tossed and turned, and great beads of sweat rolled from his brow. One moment he was awakened by his own silent scream, the next he drifted back to the unwelcome world of ghastly dreams.

Tap...tap...tap...

With startled suddenness, Dar'ock lurched from his cruel bed, snatched up his dagger, and stumbled across the room, cursing as he went. He threw open the door, and instantly fell silent. Yennea stood there, chin hanging low, tears streaming down her flushed cheeks. Dar'ock quelled his rage. With a gentle touch he reached out and wiped away a teardrop.

"Why has your smile fled, and your laughter ceased, little one?" But he didn't wait for an answer. He glanced up and down the hall, then pulled Yennea into the room and shut the door. For some reason he had expected the hunter to be at his door, not Yennea.

The girl swiped the back of her hand across her wet cheeks, and looked up into Dar'ock's face. "My mistress is dead. And the dungeon keeper has taken her to the place of sad voices."

Dar'ock arched a puzzled eyebrow. "What do you care that your mistress has died? She was an evil woman, and certainly not worthy of your tears."

Yennea sniffled, took out a hankie and wiped at her nose, and drew her brow to wrinkles. "But, are not all people worthy of tears?"

Dar'ock gaped at Yennea. He felt ill-at-ease and made no attempt to answer her question. Then, from out in the courtyard, he heard the taunting caw of the raven. Dar'ock glanced toward the window. His brow folded into tight layers, and angst moiled in his eyes. "We must leave this place, Yennea. Venomous as the enchantress was, her presence protected us. Our lives may be in danger now that she is dead. Come, daughter of Seth!"

Dar'ock swept Yennea from her feet, opened the door, and glanced one direction then the other. And with Yennea draped in his arms, he dashed noiselessly down the hall. At the sound of approaching footsteps he darted into the shadow of an alcove, and gently held his hand over Yennea's mouth. The girl did not resist. Her little body trembled. Moments later the hunter tromped by, sword in hand. A broad shouldered man, wearing a black hood, and carrying a formidable looking ax, marched at his heels. Once the harbingers of death passed from sight, Dar'ock hurried to the livery, saddled Ebony, mounted, caught up Yennea, and bolted from the stable at a gallop. At the fortress gate dirt flew everywhere as he reined in the great stallion. Dar'ock sprang from Ebony's back, ran up the narrow stairway to the gear house and manually turned the wench that lifted the portcullis. The cumbrous iron gate rose slowly.

"Hurry, Dar'ock!" Panic edged Yennea's cry.

Dar'ock blocked the gear and shot back down the stairs. The hunter and the man wearing the black hood, probably the dungeon keeper, came thundering across the lawn. Dar'ock swung up behind Yennea, and gave Ebony his heels. He looked over his shoulder and saw the hunter notch an arrow to his bow. Dar'ock leaned over Yennea and pressed Ebony to fly for the forest. The hunter's arrow swished past Dar'ock's ear. A moment later trees blurred to the right and the left. Dar'ock urged Ebony on. The forest swallowed them momentarily, and then spewed them out onto the green sward leading up toward the Way.

Dar'ock dismounted at the entrance to the tunnel, handed the reins to Yennea, slapped the stallion on the rump, and sent horse and rider racing toward freedom. Dar'ock waited inside the passageway for the hunter and the dungeon keeper to emerge from among the trees. They sprinted up the hill, and Dar'ock turned and ran through the tunnel snuffing out torch after torch. He had extinguished eight cressets when he heard the clamor of his pursuers' feet. He snuffed out one more lamp and fled like a deer chased by dogs. He dashed passed one torch, two, and then three. SWISH! An arrow ripped through the shoulder of his coat. Four torches. Five torches. KABOOM! Engulfed in flames and pummeled by flying rock, Dar'ock tumbled head over heels, slammed into the wall, whorled along the marble-like floor on his back, came to his feet, and bolted toward the eye of the tunnel. Behind him he heard the crack and crash of falling granite. Hair singed, covered with dust, and wracked with pain, Dar'ock burst from the dark hole. As he did, the earth shuddered casting him to the ground. He regained his footing. The earth shook again cracking the granite beneath him. Two strides ahead a much larger rift appeared. Yennea stood beyond the break, wide eyed, holding the sides of her head, and screaming. Dar'ock leaped the fissure, grabbed the girl, and shook her. "Yennea! Stop it!"

Tears spilled down Yennea's cheeks. She fought for control, snuffled, gaped at Dar'ock, and blurted. "You look awful! Are you all right?"

Dar'ock glanced over his shoulder. Dust boiled from the black hole. Dar'ock's mouth twisted into a self-satisfied smile. "I'll be fine, daughter of Seth." He caught her up in his arms, and carried her out beyond the boulder that shielded the gate. And there stood Garfe, his brow drawn, his eyes asking questions, and Ebony in his charge. The stallion skittered nervously. Garfe stroked the steed's lathered neck, and whispered calming words. Five other grim faced cave dwellers stood atop boulders off to the side of the trail, and watched.

Dar'ock set Yennea on her feet. The girl wrapped herself tight to his waist. Dar'ock understood her fear. After all, it was these wild men who had stolen Yennea from her home and delivered her to the hunter. Dar'ock laid a comforting and protective hand on her shoulder.

Garfe stepped forward. Dar'ock tensed.

"No man return from the Way, except giant man who does for enchantress." Dismay edged Garfe's voice. He forced a half smile. "But Garfe knew Dar'ock come back, so Garfe wait here with watchers. But why Dar'ock make it, and not others?"

"Because I was determined to disappoint you, Garfe!" A smirk etched his face. The cave dweller's eyes flared. Dar'ock laughed. And as he did, it dawned on him that he had not laughed like this since the night the enchantress had come to his bed-chamber. At the thought of Deva, Dar'ock's laughter broke off, and a pensive frown drooped his face. He looked down at Yennea and cast a fleeting look back toward the gate. "Garfe, you and your people don't have to worry about the enchantress, there will be no more sacrifices for the goddess. Deva is dead. And the Way to the land of death is closed."

Garfe's eyes flashed doubt. He squinted at Dar'ock, and drew his cheeks back in disbelief. He turned to the watchers and chattered incoherently. The cave dwellers' primitive spears came to the ready. Garfe handed Dar'ock Ebony's reins and ran past the boulder to the gate. Dar'ock could hear the echo of the troglodyte's bare, leathery feet as he padded into the tunnel. The padding became faint, and grew loud again. Garfe skittered from behind the boulder, and motioned frantically to the other cave dwellers. Two of the watchers leaped down and padded at Garfe's heels back to the Way.

Dar'ock lifted Yennea to the great stallion's saddle and swung up behind her. Four more watchers appeared, seemingly out of nowhere, blocking Dar'ock's way with their spears. The man in black acknowledged them with a nod, and waited. A few moments later Garfe and the two cave men reappeared carrying a huge sword. Garfe held the weapon high above his head, and shouted, "Giant man dead! The Way closed. Mountain drop. Tunnel pile of rocks."

The watchers all broke out in broad smiles, their eyes sparkled. Up on one of the boulders a barrel chested cave dweller turned and shouted unintelligible words that carried out across the vast gulch. A few moments later a wild cheer rose from the desolate canyon, and echoed from wall to wall. With a sweeping glance Dar'ock examined the rock-strewn waste, and wondered how many troglodytes were out there. He saw only the watchers at hand.

Dar'ock turned again, and was taken aback to see Garfe gaping at him with awe-filled eyes. And his amazement grew when the cave dweller stepped forward, arms extended, offering him the Nephilim's sword.

The man in black swung his leg back over Ebony's rump, and lowered himself to the ground. He accepted the sword from the obeisant cave dweller who, in turn, meekly bent his head toward the earth. Dar'ock stood there a moment, as if ruminating on what to do next. The corner of his mouth twitched upward, and light flickered in his eyes. He walked past Garfe and the watchers, back toward the tunnel. Garfe and his companions followed. Ebony clomped after. Dar'ock stepped across the three-foot crack in the earth, and stopped where the narrow chink in the bedrock sliced across the entrance to the Way.

Yennea and the cave men watched as Dar'ock raised the great sword, and with a powerful thrust, drove it down into the narrow rift. Metal screeched against rock as the sword lodged in place."The Keeper of the Way!" Declared Dar'ock.

Garfe and the watchers bobbed their heads and shook their spears in approval, then retreated to the shadow of the nearby boulder, and huddled in energetic conversation. When the muttering finally subsided, the watchers returned to Dar'ock, and each cave dweller reached out and touched the man in black on the chest and padded off to join their tribesmen somewhere out in the canyon. As the echo of slapping feet died away, Garfe stepped forward and extended his hand to Dar'ock's chest as well.

"What's that all about?" Yennea addressed her question to Dar'ock.

"A gesture indicating that they hold me in high esteem, I presume for the service I rendered by killing the hunter and shutting the gate."

Garfe nodded and once again dipped his head toward the ground. "Watchers go to our people, and tell them giant is dead, that our children are safe. Garfe grateful to Dar'ock, son of Cain. Garfe Dar'ock's faithful guide dog." The cave dweller gestured for Dar'ock to put the choker chain around his neck.

"No, Garfe." Dar'ock turned and took the reins from Yennea. "I will not put the chain on your neck, nor will I tie your hands and feet again. But if you want to travel with us you are welcome to do so, but not as my slave."

Dar'ock swung into the saddle and pulled Yennea up behind him, where she held tightly to his tattered coat. Garfe rubbed the scarred side of his head, looked out to where the watchers had disappeared, shrugged his shoulders and pivoted on his heels. He motioned for Dar'ock to follow.

Chapter 7
Quest for the god

And the God planted a garden eastward in Eden. And he placed a Cherubim at the east of the Garden of Eden, and a flaming sword to guard the way to the tree of life. The Book of Beginnings

Garfe led Dar'ock and Yennea to a little used trail that ran northward along the base of the great rock wall. The path eventually brought them to a recess in the palisade where the cured hide of the fangcat Dar'ock had killed lay stretched between wooden pegs driven into the hard earth.

"Camp here?" Garfe looked to the man in black for approval.

Dar'ock glanced from the small grotto, along the edge of the high wall, and then over his shoulder out across to the canyon floor. He nodded and eased Yennea down to the ground.

"What are you going to do with that hide, wild man?" Dar'ock motioned toward the skin.

"Gift for giant man." Garfe growled the words as if they were distasteful. He looked up at Dar'ock, and a broad smile spread his face. "But now I give to Son of Cain."

"I accept your gift, Garfe." Dar'ock swung down from Ebony and tethered him to a bush rooted in a crack in the cliff, and then set about lighting a fire. Yennea stood beside him shivering.

"Daughter of Seth, you're as cold as that fangcat's blood. A different world this side of the wall, isn't it?"

Yennea looked up at him and twisted her purple lips into a smile. Dar'ock frowned in return. "Your teeth are chattering, your skin is as blue as the sky, and all you've got to wear is that threadbare dress. We'll have to do something about that."

Dar'ock wrapped the shivering girl in his bedroll, and then put his knife to the hide Garfe had just given him.

With a bone needle and cured gut he stitched a pair of britches and coat. Within a couple hours Yennea was up, flitting about, and laughing again. Dar'ock watched, and wondered, "Is this strange sense of satisfaction the same a parent might feel?"

Dar'ock cast the thought aside and turned to Garfe. "Wild man, what do you think of the outfit?" He swept a hand toward Yennea.

Garfe glanced at the girl's outfit, shrugged his shoulders, then met her eye to eye. Lines creased his brow as he studied her. "Eyes like sky. Straw-colored hair. Garfe remember girl-child. Watchers give her to giant man many, many days ago." A silly looking grin spread across Garfe's face. "Garfe glad girl-child return from the Way with Son of Cain."

At Garfe's words a look of surprise passed across Yennea's face. The caveman reached out and touched her hair. Yennea smiled in return.

"You not afraid of Garfe." The cave dweller tilted his head to the side, and stared questioningly.

"Why should I fear you, Garfe? You're a friend of Dar'ock's."

Dar'ock jacked an eyebrow, waved the palm of his hand toward Yennea, and broke into the conversation. "Hold on now, daughter of Seth, I never called the wild man a friend."

Garfe looked from one to the other and grinned. He seemed to have no idea what they were talking about. Yennea shot Dar'ock a biting glance.

Dar'ock scowled. "Humph! Garfe probably doesn't even know what a friend is. I've been told wild men don't use the word. Fact is, for the most part troglodytes leave each other alone. It's said they only work together when it's to their mutual benefit, like with the watchers, but they don't actually relate to each other as friends. Now in this case, Garfe has chosen to travel with me, but that's not what you call being friends." He glanced at Garfe and grinned. "Though I must say, our relationship is a bit more congenial now than in the past."

Yennea followed Dar'ock's eyes to the scarlet scar on the side of the troglodyte's head. She wrinkled her nose in puzzlement. "Garfe, what happened to your ear?"

Garfe glowered at Dar'ock, grunted something unintelligible. He turned and walked away without giving an answer.

Yennea pressed Dar'ock with a questioning look.

"A long story, little one." He gave Yennea a wink, squatted by the campfire, and set to fanning the flame. And neither he nor Garfe would say more about the missing ear.

Night came, and the morning. Dar'ock mounted Ebony, set Yennea in front of him, gave Garfe a nod, and they were on their way. The cave dweller drubbed his feet along a trail so little used that it seemed almost nonexistent, but he never hesitated. He padded along and Ebony followed. Dar'ock sat straight in the saddle, always alert and watching. Yennea, on the other hand, slumbered, leaning on the saddle horn. When she tilted suddenly to one side or the other Dar'ock would tip her upright again. Near midmorning she yawned, stretched her arms, and came back to life.

"Look!" Yennea pointed toward a narrow ledge that traced a line up the side of the granite escarpment. "That's not where we're going, is it?"

Garfe looked over his shoulder, and spread a toothy grin. "No problem. Trail solid rock. Girl-child not worry."

Yennea looked up at Dar'ock. The corner of his mouth twitched into a slight grin, he lifted his eyebrows, and gave Ebony rein. Yennea sighed. And so they began the climb up the perilous track. Yennea clamped white knuckled hands to the saddle horn.

Half way up the high wall Garfe shot a furtive look back at Dar'ock.

"So what's your problem, wild man?"

Garfe beetled his bushy brows. "After leave canyon, where going? Garfe, not want to go to Nod. People of Nod not like Garfe's people. Garfe not safe there."

"Nod?" Dar'ock shook his head. "Actually, Garfe, it's said that our eldest forefather, Adam, walked with the god in a place called Eden."

The caveman's face went white. "Garfe rather go to Nod! Eden forbidden place. Shining warrior there. No man allowed to enter."

"Forbidden?" Dar'ock gazed back toward the Way. "We'll see."

"Dar'ock not find the god in Eden." Garfe stared at the man in black. "Maybe he only find trouble there."

"Seems to me I find trouble wherever I go, wild man." He heaved his shoulders. "Anyway, I'm going in search of Eden, and you can go with me, or venture where you will."

Garfe wagged his head, turned back to the trail and continued on.

"What do you think daughter of Seth?" Dar'ock turned his attention to Yennea. "Will we find the god at Eden?"

"I heard my mother and father speak of Eden, but I don't remember what they said, except that it was a garden. But, you don't have to go to Eden to find the God. My father used to say that he is everywhere near."

Dar'ock glanced about in an exaggerated manner and waved a hand in a sweeping arc. "Well, if the god is everywhere near, why can't I see him? Perhaps he is hiding down there with the watchers!"

"I was told you cannot see God unless he chooses to let you."

"I suppose you see him?" Dar'ock chided.

Yennea smiled. "I see him with my heart."

"Foolish girl, the god you speak of is but a figment of your imagination. The god I pursue is not a ghost hiding in the shadows. No the god I seek has substance."

Yennea bobbed her blond curls. "No, Dar'ock, it is your god that does not exist. He isn't big enough to be God."

Dar'ock's mood turned dark and he spouted profanities.

Yennea twisted about and looked up at him. A hint of anger burned in her eyes. "You asked me what I thought."

"So I did, Daughter of Seth. But the fact is, I don't really care what you think!" And with that he fell silent.

They tramped upward for some time before Dar'ock broke the quiet. "Daughter of Seth? You've said nothing about returning to your village and family. Don't you desire to go home?"

"I don't know where home is." Yennea's spirit drooped. "Besides, my mistress told me I don't have a family anymore."

"Maybe the watchers could help us..."

Garfe broke in before Dar'ock could finish. "Not good to talk about girl-child's village. Dar'ock girl-child's family."

"I'm her family? Garfe, we've got to..."

Garfe shot a fiery glance over his shoulder, grated his teeth, and made a gesture as if smashing something with a club.

"I see, wild man." Dar'ock grimaced and looked down at the girl. "I guess the enchantress was right, Daughter of Seth."

"Then you're my family?"

"Humph! I do suppose Garfe and I are as much family as you have right now. So I guess you will have to go with us in search of the god."

Garfe shot Dar'ock a peevish glance. "Dumb thing!" he growled.

"Call it dumb if you like, wild man, but we're going looking for the god."

Chapter 8
The Waresman

Lamech took two wives. One was Zillah. And Zillah bore Tubal-Cain, an instructor of every craftsman in bronze and iron. The Book of Beginnings

It was late afternoon when they reached the brim of the canyon, where they came to a broad trail that skirted the rim of the high wall north and south. Garfe turned to the south.

"Hold up, wild man." Dar'ock reined in Ebony. "Someone comes from the north. Let's see who treks this godforsaken high country."

Yennea looked up at him, and her eyes told him she didn't much care for his choice of words. "Well, I don't see the god around here anywhere." He muttered.

The sound that had reached Dar'ock's ears became more distinct, the clatter of metal clanging against metal. Not the clamor of drawn swords, but rather the rattle of pots banging pans.

Moments later a broad shouldered man with a bushy red beard came trundling along the trail. The waresman wore a brimless fur hat, pulled down over his ears, animal hide britches, and a heavy fur coat. A sad looking, but stout legged, swayback brown horse, laden with chattels, followed the lead that dangled from the trader's hand. As if in protest of its labor the horse puffed and snorted as it plodded along. Behind the cob trudged a diminutive fellow with stumpy legs, a squat body, and hunched shoulders. He wasn't much taller than Yennea. He walked with his face to the ground. But the most striking thing about the strange little man was that he had no hair, and both scalp and chin looked scarred.

As the red haired trader approached, he cast Garfe and Dar'ock a wary eye.

"So peddler, do you travel the high country looking to sell your wares to cave dwellers?" The crease of Dar'ock's face was more cynical grin than smile. "Or perhaps you have a death wish and have come to be their prey?"

The man's scowl thawed, and he laughed boldly. "Worry not, stranger, I can take care of myself!" He lifted a leather cord that flaunted ten or more shaggy black scalps. Garfe's eyes narrowed and he grated his teeth noisily. Being ignorant of the ways of men, Yennea stared as if having no idea what the furry things were. Dar'ock took note when the trader lifted the scalps that the little man, or pip, as such were called, put his hands to his head and cowered.

"So you've traveled this path before." Dar'ock returned his attention to the waresman. He nodded toward the string of pelts. "I didn't realize that the Sons of Seth engaged in barbaric practices."

The peddler's laughter stopped. Fire kindled in his eyes, the corner of his mouth twitched nervously, and with but what seemed like a slight stir, a glinting battleax appeared in his hand.

The little hunchback who stood at a distance began to quaver. Garfe stepped back from the peddler, continuing his guttural growl. Yennea pushed back hard against Dar'ock's chest. But the man in black didn't flinch. He grinned, cocked an eyebrow, and trolled, "Easy friend, I meant no offense by my words. And besides, why should you die before you've reached your destination?" He smiled down at the trader. The air turned heavy as the potential combatants measured each other. The man in black broke the silence.

"I'm Dar'ock, Prince of Nod. My friends and I are traveling to Eden in search of the god. So, merchant, what brings you to the high country?"

The fur clad traveler feigned laughter. The fire in his eyes died to flashing embers. "You live dangerously, Prince of Nod. I'm Poygr the Peddler. Perhaps you have heard of me?"

"Yes, but in Nod they call you Poygr the Barbarian. You are not well liked in Nod, Poygr."

The peddler beamed, as if pleased with the report. "I am not well liked anywhere, Prince of Nod. But I survive. And due to the kindness of my barbaric heart I shall let you live to see another day as well."

"Thank you for your benevolence, Poygr." Dar'ock motioned to the right with a nod of his head. "We're going to make camp to the south, near the forest. You and your slave are welcome to join us for the evening."

Poygr accepted Dar'ock's invitation. Garfe shot Dar'ock an angry glance, and sputtered a line of foul words. Yennea looked up over her shoulder at Dar'ock. Lines of concern etched her brow. Dar'ock ignored both Garfe and Yennea.

And so, with wares banging and clanging, Poygr led his sniggering old swayback on toward the south. His deformed drudge followed, wringing his hands, and nervously glancing up at the other travelers as he passed. Garfe waited for Dar'ock to rein Ebony in behind the peddler's slave and trailed at a safe distance.

They passed through a breadth of scabland before coming to rugged hill country scattered with trees. The forest thickened and dropped down to the crest of a bluff that edged the trail. They continued on to where the bluff recessed back from the road. There a cave opening beckoned.

"Well, Prince of Nod, this looks like as good a place as any. Wouldn't you say?" Poygr tethered his sway-back to a sapling at the base of the tor. As he walked away the cob flared its nostrils and exhaled loudly.

Dar'ock reined in Ebony, and let his eyes scan the area. "It'll do, peddler."

Poygr's drudge set to easing the poor pack horse's burden, though not without a curse or two from his master for being clumsy or slow, or both. The pip quailed, but kept at the task.

Even when Poygr turned to walk away, he continued to badger the poor drudge. "Majet, if you dent one of those pots, I'll dent the side of your head with my ax. You're as graceless an oaf as you are stupid! And don't be all day about your doin'. The four-legger don't seem to have much poop left in him. If ya cross me I'll have you carry my wares tomorrow."

Poygr laughed obnoxiously. No one laughed with him.

Dar'ock gave the peddler an expressionless glance, not so much precipitated by the waresman's words or laughter, as the need to keep an eye on the fellow. He dropped some dry sticks in the fire pit just outside the entrance to the cave. "Poygr's familiar with this place," he mused to himself. He hunkered down and busied himself lighting the campfire.

Yennea sat on a nearby log and watched Dar'ock whittle a stick into shavings. Poygr walked by Yennea, reached out and fondled her dangling curls. She pulled away. Anger momentarily twisted the waresman's face, but it passed quickly. He stepped back and let his eyes peruse her head to foot. "The girl for sale?" he grunted. Ignoring her obvious discomfort he reached out and again fingered one of her curls, and waited for Dar'ock's response. The air fell heavy with silence. Poygr shifted and met Dar'ock's simmering stare. "Just asking. If she's not for sale, what do I care." The peddler let Yennea's hair spill from his hand, and strayed back over to where Majet prepared a feedbag for the swayback. The peddler swatted the pip upside the head. "Don't overdo it, fool! Snort don't need to feast at my expense. If the feed don't last till we get to the next town he'll be eatin' your food!"

Majet writhed into a tight little ball, and scurried off, feed bag in hand, to where Snort was tethered.

Dar'ock ignored the whole scene. As far as he was concerned that was just the way a slave was treated. Nothing to get excited about! Garfe, on the other hand, watching from the dark of the cave issued a low, guttural growl. Yennea cowered and wiped a tear from her eye.

Later, the travelers sat around the fire and shared a sparse meal. In the midst of the repast Dar'ock brought up the matter of his quest, and inquired as to the way to Eden.

"You will not find the god in Eden." The peddler cocked an eyebrow, and cast Dar'ock a twisted smile and wiped his mouth on the back of his hand. "The god walks there no longer. But there is a place you might find him, a city I once visited."

"And what city might that be?" Irritation edged Dar'ock's voice. He had a plan, and he wasn't prone to changing it, at least not at the peddler's prompting.

Poygr shot Dar'ock a peevish glare. "It's called the Hidden City, if you really want to know. But what do I care if you waste your time trekkin' off to Eden."

Tension filled the air like the brewing of a storm. And it didn't help that the peddler's gaze kept shifting to Dar'ock's hair.

"Ok, peddler, for the sake of argument, if the god's not at Eden, why would he be visiting the Hidden City?" Dar'ock recognized the name of the town, but had heard nothing about the god ever having been there.

"Well, I certainly didn't see him there!" Mockery rode Poygr's words. "But I traded wares at the gate of the Hidden City with an old man named Methuselah. Now, old Methuselah had a son named Enoch, and word in those parts has it that at eventide the people of the city actually saw the old man's son walking with the god out across the grasslands. And not infrequently either. Why, old Methuselah himself told me the god was so taken with the fellow that one day he just snatched him away to the City of the God. Not that I believe it, of course."

"Interesting." Dar'ock remained skeptical. He gazed at the fire lost in thought. When he looked up he caught Poygr once again eyeing his hair. The peddler instantly shifted his gaze to Yennea. His eyes lingered, and then he turned back to Dar'ock and continued his story.

"Now, I've never been to the City of the God, and have no desire to go there. A blind soothsayer once told me that it lies somewhere beyond Eden in the far reaches of the land of Seth. If such a city actually does exist, that's where you'll find the god. But the Hidden City is the place to begin. The soothsayer is dead now, so you'll want to look up an old man named Methuselah. Strange old cuss, but if anyone can tell you where the City of the God is, it's him. And if he can't, well, no one can!"

"Thank you, peddler. Now, tell me another story." Dar'ock nodded toward Poygr's slave who sat over by the merchant's wares. "We've been together half a day now, and your grunt there hasn't spoken a word. Is he mute or does he not speak the language?"

Poygr looked over at Majet, then turned to Dar'ock, and with eye deceiving speed he drew a double edged knife and sliced air with the blade. He showed all his teeth, and laughed a rigid, caustic laugh, if laugh it could be called. "Caught the little humpy trying to rob my wares one night when I was traveling through the Valley of Dead Trees. Skinned his head on the spot, and left him for dead. But the next morning there he was, head and face matted with blood, but still alive. Yes sir, that humpy's a real scrapper!

"Well, I decided that since the pip had tried to steal my goods, I'd make him spend the rest of his days guarding them. And wouldn't you know, the halfwit had the gall to complain. Jabbered on and on about my being cruel. Put up with it for a day or two, but got tired of his chatter!" The peddler's blade flashed in a twisting motion. "Cut out his tongue. Now the pip gives me no trouble, and that's the way I like it."

Garfe growled. Poygr's face flushed with rage, and his dagger trembled.

"Easy, Poygr." Dar'ock spoke softly, and motioned with a backward flick of his hand toward Garfe, encouraging him to put some distance between himself and the peddler. "Garfe is a bit sensitive about that subject. You noticed he's missing an ear. You can be sure his grunting is directed toward me rather than you. He's untamed, but like your pip, he's harmless."

Poygr formed his lips into a smile, but Dar'ock could see that a fire still burned. On the other hand, neither he nor Poygr noticed the tear on Yennea's cheek. Nor did they take note of Majet's dispirited countenance.

Dar'ock gestured toward the road, and cast the peddler a questioning glance. "On the morrow we go our separate ways. Against my better judgment, I've decided to take your advice, and travel to the Hidden City. Perhaps this Methuselah fellow can aid my quest. And where are you off to, peddler?"

"I go where I go." Poygr lifted his mug of brew and saluted Dar'ock. A mischievous grin parted the peddler's bushy red beard, and his eyes shifted nervously. "And you, Prince of Nod, may you live to see the old man's face."

Dar'ock ran his fingers through his hair. He offered a broad smirk. "I shall, peddler, and thank you for the favorable omen."

Chapter 9
Poor Majet

And the God was sorry that he had made the men of the earth, and their deeds grieved the God to his heart. The Book of Beginnings

*T*wilight passed, and darkness came. Dar'ock tossed several sticks on the dying fire. Soon shadows danced on the face of the bluff, and in the branches of nearby trees. Dar'ock shined his silver pipe and touched the night with a woeful strain that gave Poygr cause to grimace.

The palled merchant got up and checked on his drudge, who lay sleeping outside by the pile of pots and pans, and then the peddler retreated into the depths of the cave with a heavy wool blanket in hand. Garfe and Yennea slept outside the cave under the lip of the bluff.

Dar'ock finished his dirge, then retired to the mouth of the cave, where he placed himself between Yennea and the unseen peddler who lay somewhere back in the inky blackness. And as Dar'ock laid out his wrap, the caw of a raven broke the night. He turned and peered out toward the stand of trees near the rim of the canyon, and then shifted his gaze to the deeper dark inside the cave. He grinned, leaned back against the stone wall, wrapped himself in his coat, and waited. As time passed, Dar'ock's eyes grew heavy and sleep overtook him.

As the night deepened the fire became but a few smoldering embers. Now and again a coal would pop, and break the stillness of the night. Wearing soft fur boots, Poygr moved noiselessly across the rock floor. The head skinner's eyes blazed with passion. His gnarled grin spoke insolence and blood lust. The ax in his hand, catching the light of the rising moon, glimmered cold and terrible. He stopped just short of the sleeping prince, and slowly lifted his razor edged weapon. Steel flashed in the night. The peddler's eyes went wide, as the blade of Dar'ock's dagger rived his chest bone and drove deep. The peddler's ax clattered on the stone floor. He wilted to his knees clutching his chest, sucking air.

"I say, Poygr, looks like you've met your match," Dar'ock grated quietly.

The moment Poygr's ax hit the cave floor, Garfe sprang to his feet, ready to flee into the night.

"Easy, wild man! It's all right, our friend here is enjoying his last breath of air," Dar'ock whispered. He laid a finger to his lips. "Don't wake Yennea. She doesn't need to see this."

Poygr gaped at the man in black, shuddered, and went limp. Dar'ock let him slip from the blade to the ground. He picked up the head skinner's ax and handed it to Garfe.

"Hmm. Nice weapon." Garfe ran a finger along the side of the blade, carefully avoiding the edge.

With effort, Dar'ock dragged Poygr out to the rim of the canyon and edged him over. "Heavier than I expected," he huffed as he watched the peddler disappear down into darkness. He sighed and returned to the cave. He passed by Majet who stood by the peddler's wares, his face sheeted with terror, and his hands shaking at his mouth.

"Forget what you saw, pip," Dar'ock snarled. Majet stumbled backward over the supplies. "And discard that junk back in the cave." Dar'ock turned and passed on to where the waresman had fallen, dusted the pool of blood with dirt and rocks, and returned to his sleep.

Garfe slinked over to Majet, helped him to his feet, and assured him he had nothing to fear. "Dar'ock not hurt little man, unless little man give him reason." He shook his head. "Little man's master gave Dar'ock reason. Peddler not smart to fool with Dar'ock. No, that not smart at all. But little man not dumb. He come with Garfe. Garfe take care of him. Garfe civilized."

Majet motioned toward the dead peddler's wares. Garfe cocked an eyebrow and spread his hands, indicating he did not understand. Majet picked up a couple of items and offered them to Garfe, and then pointed at the pile.

"You want Garfe take something?"

Majet nodded. Garfe grinned, glanced over toward Dar'ock, then quietly rummaged about to see if he could find something useful. Dar'ock watched momentarily, then turned away and sought for sleep. Yennea slept soundly through the whole ordeal.

When the morning sun beckoned the travelers to wakefulness, the pots and pans were gone, and of course, Poygr did not join them for breakfast. Yennea expressed concern.

"Perhaps the peddler slipped away during the night." Dar'ock showed little concern for Poygr's absence.

"Without his horse?" Yennea cast Dar'ock a reproving look.

"Odd, isn't!" Dar'ock cocked an eyebrow at Garfe. "Did you see the peddler leave, wild man?"

"Garfe, hear him moving about in the night. Maybe peddler had to relieve self of much brew he drank last night."

Dar'ock looked about, and then walked over to the edge of the canyon. Far below Poygr's body lay sprawled on the rocks. "What do you know! Looks like our merchant friend prowled too close to the escarpment and fell to his death."

Yennea hurried to Dar'ock's side. She held his arm and looked down at the canyon floor. "How awful!" she gasped.

"Very bad!" murmured Garfe. Then using a word he had learned from Dar'ock, he added, "But at least poor barbarian take no more scalps."

"What will we do with him?" A tear trickled down Yennea's cheek. She wiped it away. Deep inside she struggled with confusion. She felt sadness at the peddler falling to his death, but at the same time she felt relieved that he was gone. She hurriedly pushed aside her bewilderment. "And poor Majet; he's lost his master."

Dar'ock glanced over at the pip who sat under the edge of the bluff. The look on Majet's face indicated unwillingness to come and see.

"Do with the peddler?" Dar'ock looked back down to the canyon floor, then turned and walked away. "Don't worry, little one, the wild will take care of him."

"But we can't just leave him down there, for animals to feed on!" Yennea's voice faltered. "We must take him to his people!"

The man in black laughed. "Poygr had no people. And even if he did, his body would rot before we could get him there. Have you ever smelled sun baked flesh? Well, you don't want to!"

Dar'ock's thoughts instantly went to Deva's Dungeon. He shuddered.

Yennea stuck her hands to her hips. "Then we must bury him."

The Prince of Nod rolled his eyes and gritted his teeth impatiently. "And are you going to climb down and haul his body up here? And when you haul it up where do you propose we bury it? Even the trees of the forest cling to bedrock."

"We can bury him down there with big stones."

"I can't believe my ears!" Dar'ock motioned toward the rim of the canyon. "If we had twenty strands of rope we still could not get down to the peddler's sorry carcass, and we're not taking two extra days to go back down the trail we came up." He shot a peevish glance at the rising sun. "It's time to leave. Pack up your bedroll."

Yennea opened her mouth to protest.

"I don't want to hear it!" growled Dar'ock as he spun on his heels and headed back over to the cave. Yennea looked once more at the distant body, sighed deeply, went over and folded her bedroll, then sat on a rock out by the trail with her chin slumped on the heel of her hand.

Garfe disappeared inside the cave. He emerged dressed in brown leather britches, a hide vest, and carrying Poygr's ax. Dar'ock stared in disbelief. Majet grinned in approval. Yennea commented somberly, "Much better, Garfe."

The troglodyte stuck out his chest. "Garfe, civilized son of Cain."

Dar'ock grinned. Yennea could not help letting out a slight giggle. Majet nodded vigorously.

Fussing and fumbling about, Garfe put the weapon in its sheath and tried to gird the sheath to his torso. Finally Majet strolled over and strapped it on for him, stood back, set his hands to his hips, cocked an eyebrow, and gave Garfe an affirming nod. Garfe returned Majet's approval by reaching out and touching his chest.

Dar'ock brought the peddler's swayback out to the trail. He extended Snort's reins toward Yennea. "Here, he's smaller and gentler than Ebony, so you should be able to handle him just fine."

Yennea's mouth dropped open and her eyes went wide. "We can't take Poygr's horse. It wouldn't be right."

"Look, girl, would you have the poor beast stay here and starve, or become food for a fangcat, or some cave dweller's family?" Dar'ock stuck the reins in Yennea's hand. "The peddler is dead. The least you can do for him is take care of his horse."

Behind Yennea Garfe raised his eyebrows, and gave Dar'ock a look that said, "As if you really care!"

"If anyone is to have Poygr's horse it should be poor Majet." Yennea looked over her shoulder to the pip, who now faithfully tagged at Garfe's heels.

"Majet has no interest in the beast, avoids him when he can." Dar'ock set his jaw. "So if you aren't going to take responsibility for Snort, we'll leave him to fend for himself here in the wild."

Yennea sighed, looked from Dar'ock to Snort, who at that very moment hanged his head, flared his nostrils, and puffed air. Snort then gave Yennea the saddest of looks.

"Well, I don't know how to ride a horse by myself, but I will do my best." She stood and slowly approached the poor cob. "But what if he doesn't want to be ridden?"

"If he could handle all those wares Poygr piled on his back, he certainly won't mind having you sitting there, little one."

Yennea rubbed Snort's neck. "Of course, I'll have to change his name. Snort seems an awful name for a horse."

Dar'ock tossed the peddler's wool blanket over Snort's back. "Give the critter any name you like. But be quick about it. We've already wasted half the morning. It's time to move on."

"Very well then, I shall call him Poger."

Dar'ock's face pulled into a tight-lipped scowl. He grated his teeth as he wrapped a makeshift cinch around blanket and horse, then turned and faced Yennea. "You can give this animal any name but that one, daughter of Seth. Poger is much too close to Poygr, and that's a name I'd rather not be reminded of on a regular basis."

"You said I could give him any name I wished, and Poger is the name I have given him, in honor of the poor peddler." Yennea's gaze did not give way to Dar'ock's glare. She smiled, shrugged a shoulder, and patted the horse on its nose. "His name is Poger, and that's that!"

"You are an obstinate child!" Dar'ock grated out the words as he hoisted Yennea to the horse's back. "Poger it is. But now, let me give you some basic instructions about riding this beast. Although he's used to carrying a load, the old sway has probably never been ridden, which means he may not be trained to respond to commands."

Yennea nudged the gelding with her heels. Poger just stood there. "Go horse!" she urged. Nothing. Yennea kicked a bit harder, though not nearly hard enough. But the only response she got was a snort and a snuff. She snapped the gelding's rump with the reins, but too gently to have any effect. Poger looked back at Yennea as if amused by her gestures. Dar'ock shook his head, took back the reins and tied them to a ring in Ebony's saddle. He mounted, turned Ebony to the trail, and Poger followed obediently. Yennea grabbed the loop Dar'ock had made in the cinch rope, and as they trekked along she chattered on about how fine a horse Poger was, and about her disappointment at leaving the poor peddler, and about whatever came to mind. Dar'ock grumbled expletives under his breath. Garfe, with Majet dogging in his tracks, led the way.

"Hidden City far away. But nice green valley lies beyond mountain." Garfe pointed toward a snow spotted peak to the east. "Garfe lead Dar'ock to nice green valley. Good place to live. Majet says six days journey, maybe seven."

"What do you mean, 'Majet says?' Majet doesn't say anything!"

"He has his ways."

"Well, I don't care what he says. We're going to the Hidden City to talk to that old man Poygr told us about." The passion of quest was back in Dar'ock's voice.

"Now, two questions. One, are you going with me? Two, do you know the way?"

Garfe's shoulders wilted, and glumness weighted his voice. "Humph! Garfe go with Dar'ock. Maybe turn back later." He shook his head and pointed a thumb toward the pip. "Garfe not know way to far off place, but Majet know. He tell Garfe, and Garfe lead Dar'ock."

Majet turned to look at the man in black. The pip's eyes sparkled, and his face shined. He was obviously enjoying his new role better than his old one.

"Dar'ock?" called out Yennea. "How long will it take us to get to the Hidden City?"

The man in black shifted in his saddle. "Long, daughter of Seth, long."

Chapter 10
Vale of Mourning

"So now you are cursed from the earth!" And Cain said to the God, "My punishment is greater than I can bear!" The Book of Beginnings

*T*he four unlikely companions trekked through barren canyons, across rock-strewn flats, down into lush green valleys, alongside tumbling rivers, back up along narrow ledges, and over snow covered passes. The days became weeks and weeks turned into months. The inner sides of Yennea's legs ached from riding horseback, but her smile remained. Garfe mumbled words like, "Dumb waste of time! Not smart. Stupid thing!" Dar'ock paid him no mind. In every village and city they were told that the Hidden City lay somewhere farther north. Majet would nod, point, and they would continue on their way.

After leaving a town called Lasech, they met a traveler who told them that when the trail forked beyond the Donex Hills they should take the way leading north and west, but just where the Hidden City lay he did not know. Majet bobbed his head in agreement, Dar'ock thanked the traveler, and again they pressed on. They crossed the Donex Hills, and when the trail forked they veered north and west.

The sun rose, and the sun set. And as the journey lengthened, Dar'ock found himself drawn to Yennea. When he put his hands about her waist and lifted her to Poger's back or put his arm about her to help her down again, desire stirred inside. Her yellow hair tantalized. Her fine features compelled. But day after day he suppressed his passions.

"She's only a child," he reasoned.

"But a woman, nonetheless!" Passion responded. "And she's of marriageable age."

So it was that one evening, while Garfe and Majet were off scrounging for rock beetles and mountain mice, Dar'ock cast restraint aside. Ignoring Yennea's pleas, he forced himself on her. When he finished his cruelty he experienced the fullness of a feeling he had only recently come to know...guilt. He got to his feet and turned his back on Yennea.

Pain wracked the girl's body, and she wept uncontrollably. She looked up. "Why, Dar'ock?"

He refused to face her.

Yennea began to sob. "Why did you do this to me?"

"Cover yourself!" he demanded, then walked away.

Now Dar'ock did not regard the bedding of Yennea as rape. After all, he was a man. He had needs. She was a young woman. Yes, very young, but a woman nonetheless, for all intents and purposes she had become his slave, and thus, if he so chose, his concubine too. But it bothered Dar'ock that he did not feel gratified. He had never before felt angry with himself, as he did now. And he felt shame. That too was a new feeling.

Garfe and Majet returned to a somber camp. Dar'ock's mood was sullen. Yennea remained wrapped in her bedroll and refused to look at them.

"What happen to girl-child's smile?" Garfe put the question to Dar'ock, and Majet bobbed his head as if he too were asking the question.

Dar'ock glanced over at Yennea to be sure she was far enough away not to hear their conversation. "She's not well." he grated. "It's a woman thing."

Garfe grinned broadly and cocked an eyebrow at Majet, who raised both eyebrows and formed his lips as if to whistle.

Garfe turned back to Dar'ock. "Tears woman thing too?"

Dar'ock responded with an expletive and walked away.

*T*he next morning Dar'ock found himself questioning whether he should continue his quest. And it was not Garfe's badgering that bothered him. Rather, it was Yennea. Every time he looked at her his soul muttered, "I'm not sure I really wanted to find the god!" Of course, the real point of turmoil was the idea of having to face the god, but he refused to admit it, even to himself.

*S*everal days passed before Yennea recuperated sufficiently to travel. When they broke camp Dar'ock lifted himself to Ebony's back, and set the stallion to the trail behind Garfe and Majet. He looked back at Yennea who sat astride Poger sullen and quiet. It saddened Dar'ock that he saw no laughter in her eyes. "Is her smile forever gone?" he asked himself. He sighed deeply. "And, alas, I am the one who ripped it from her face." He mulled the thought for a moment, and grimaced, as he came to the realization that the joy Yennea had once bubbled with had been more wonderful to him than the short-lived indulgence of his lust. "I robbed myself as well as her," he mused as he rode along the mountain path. "I have come to care about this girl-child as if she were my daughter, and yet by a momentary selfish act I have spoiled our relationship." Dar'ock's shoulders sagged, and as he pushed onward, his passion for finding the god wilted.

Garfe used the opportunity of Dar'ock's flagging mood to once again press him to end his quest. "Nothing good will come of finding the god. The god curse sons of Cain. Dumb thing to rouse the god's anger."

Majet nodded agreement. Yennea, on the other hand, didn't seem to hear the conversation. She just stared off into space.

Dar'ock listened to Garfe's prodding, shook his head, and nodded toward the trail. His gaze was drawn to Yennea. The corners of his mouth wilted. He turned Ebony's head to the track, and followed Garfe's lead.

But two days following, when they came to a valley with floral meadows, stands of evergreen trees, and a large pristine mere, Dar'ock called the journey to a halt.

"We will make our home there." He gestured toward a knoll overlooking the small lake. "This is a fertile valley, rich with game, and fish jump in the pond. We can live here in comfort for many years."

So Dar'ock, Garfe and Majet set to work building a cabin, while a somber Yennea watched, and tended the needs of Ebony and Poger.

Then one day while Garfe cut notches with his ax, and Dar'ock and Majet stripped bark, Yennea asked a question that had been on her mind for some time. "Dar'ock, why do you no longer desire to find God?"

The corner of Dar'ock's mouth twitched. He hesitated, lifted his head and gazed at Yennea. He was surprised to find that she actually wore a slight smile. And that tiny upward twist to her lips lifted his spirit, and he realized how deeply he longed to hear the sound of her laughter again. Dar'ock sighed, he felt weary. He muttered, "You ask too many questions, Yennea!" He contemplated saying more, but thought better of it.

Garfe had stopped to listen, but quickly went back to scattering wood chips, grunting something about being glad the journey had come to an end. Garfe had often expressed that he had no desire to go to the Hidden City, and even less desire to find himself face to face with the god. It was obvious to Dar'ock that the very thought of standing before the god filled Garfe with fear. He knew that the last thing Garfe wanted was for Yennea to talk him into continuing his quest. He watched with amusement as Garfe made a ruckus, and sent a shower of chips flying in the girl's direction. Yennea backed away, and did not press the issue further. Dar'ock turned back to his work.

Later that day Yennea sat by the campfire while Dar'ock fixed the evening meal. Garfe and Majet had gone down to the mere to get water, and Dar'ock used the opportunity to ask Yennea a question that had been bothering him throughout the day.

"Daughter of Seth, for some time your face has reflected no joy." He did not look her in the eyes. "And to be honest, I have wondered if you would ever smile again. So tell me, Daughter of Seth, what is it that has caused your smile to return?"

"I have found peace in the one you no longer seek."

Dar'ock shook his head and thought, "Peace, Daughter of Seth? Your heart should be filled with hatred!" He kept the thought to himself. He glanced up into her eyes. "I envy you," he said before dropping his gaze.

A few moments later Garfe and Majet showed up sloshing a bucket of water, and proudly displaying a wiggling fish on the end of a makeshift spear. "Fish almost good as rock beetles," said Garfe. Majet jacked his head up and down in agreement. Dar'ock sent them off again to clean the fish away from camp. He sat down by the fire, took out his silver pipe, and played a questioning sort of dirge.

After a month the cabin was ready for its occupants. The four companions moved in, and Yennea set to work making the rustic cabin into a home. But three days of labor took its toll. The fourth day Yennea complained of feeling weak. The next morning she woke up feeling sick, and stayed in bed most of the day. Her sickness continued. Dar'ock watched in silence as Majet attended to Yennea's needs.

One day when Dar'ock and Yennea were alone in the cabin, he shared his thoughts concerning the cause of her sickness. "Daughter of Seth, if I'm not mistaken, you are with child."

Panic flushed Yennea's face. "I'm going to have a baby?" Yennea felt confused and frightened. Dar'ock explained, as best he could, what having a baby involved. Yennea wept for fear, and yet, deep inside she felt an inexplicable sense of joy.

The thought of having a child pleased Dar'ock. "Of course it will be a boy," he affirmed to himself. None of his four wives back in Nod had been able to bear him a son. However, he felt certain this daughter of Seth would indeed give birth to a man-child.

The months passed. Wildflowers danced to the whisper of balmy breezes. Gentle tongues licked at tottering fawns. Kits sought their mother's milk. And Yennea's time came. She did indeed give birth to a son. But the child came breech, making Yennea's labor long and arduous. It was after hours of tears, wailing, sweat and intense anguish that the boy finally lurched out into the world.

Yennea was aware of Dar'ock lifting the baby. She heard the child's cry, and Dar'ock's laughter. The corners of Yennea's mouth turned gently upward, she drew in a deep breath, and closed her eyes.

Out the corner of his eye Dar'ock saw Yennea exhale. But her chest did not rise again. Garfe and Majet stood by with hot water and a swaddling cloth. Garfe looked at Majet. Majet looked at Garfe. Both turned helpless eyes toward Dar'ock, who voiced the dread words. "She's quit breathing!" He handed the child to Garfe, who in turn passed him to Majet. Dar'ock knelt beside Yennea, and commanded her to live. A faint smile lay upon her ghost-like face, but her lips did not move, her eyes remained closed, and her breast remained motionless.

"Breathe, daughter of Seth!" Dar'ock cried, but to no avail. And for the first time in his life Dar'ock felt helpless. Tears welled in his eyes. He looked from Yennea to the little boy squirming in the pip's arms, the little boy for whom he had chosen the name Lamar, Source of Joy.

However, as Dar'ock looked on the child there was no gladness in his heart. He rose to his feet gaping at his little boy. Lamar's face seemed too drawn, his eyes lacked sparkle. And he cried, not as most children cry, but as if in pain. "The color of his skin is not right!" Dar'ock mumbled. Then he remembered the remark the Enchantress had made about the death she was dying being passed on to him, and a terrible wail rose from deep in his soul, and he lamented, "Oh, little Lamar, forgive me! Forgive me! for I have passed the death on to you!"

That day Dar'ock buried Yennea beneath the spreading branches of a benara tree, north of the cabin on the knoll overlooking the Mere of Tears, and three days later he laid Lamar to rest at her side. Dar'ock hunkered down at the base of the tree, looked out on the sparkling mere, took out his silver pipe, and mourned. Garfe and Majet watched and listened from a distance, though they did not understand his pain.

To Dar'ock everything about the valley reminded him of Yennea, and thoughts of Yennea brought images of little Lamar to mind. And so it was that the valley of their dwelling became the Vale of Mourning. Without fail, when the sun turned its face from the dell, the man in black would visit the site where Yennea and Lamar were buried, lifted the shiny flute to his lips, and lamented their passing. For three years Dar'ock's dirges greeted the darkness. And within the mournful melody of grief there resounded a counter strain of anger.

Chapter 11
Journey's End

Enoch begot Methuselah. And Enoch walked with God three hundred years, and he was not, for God took him. And Methuselah lived nine hundred and sixty-nine years; and he died. The Book of Beginnings

Although Dar'ock never talked about leaving the valley, Garfe feared that in the midst of despondency Dar'ock would decide to renew his quest to have words with the god. Garfe had noticed that Dar'ock's "playings" had changed from mournful to sullen. But Garfe avoided the subject of the quest, because he liked living in the Vale of Mourning. He liked being civilized. Garfe wore clothes, well, britches and a shirt, slept in a bed, fished, hunted and most of the time ate normal foods. Garfe even worked in the garden with Majet. The cave dweller had found his Eden. He was content. So when Dar'ock began packing for a journey, Garfe became anxious.

"Garfe, it's time to leave this valley." Dar'ock had just come in from his nightly vigil. Garfe and Majet sat in front of the fire, Majet showing Garfe how to shuck peas. Garfe's head jerked up and his thumb sent peas rolling across the floor. Majet glanced up at Dar'ock and scowled.

"Why leave nice cabin?" Garfe's tone clearly indicated that he was unhappy with Dar'ock's utterance. "Valley good place to live."

Majet grunted something indistinguishable, but clearly in agreement with Garfe. The two men went back to shucking peas, as if ignoring the issue would make it go away.

"Why are we damned for the sins of Cain, Garfe? And why did Yennea and Lamar suffer for mine?" Dar'ock flopped down onto a rustic log chair that creaked with the impact of his weight. "I long for peace, but there is none. The shadow of death dogs my heels, but for what reason? Garfe, these questions and more eat at the core of my soul. Questions for which I would have answers."

"The god curse the Sons of Cain. The god will not give Dar'ock answers. The god will laugh in Dar'ock's face."

"That may be, Garfe, but nonetheless, I will pursue him until I find him, and I will have words with the god. Yennea was a daughter of Seth. She held the god in high regard, but look what he did to her."

Garfe set his jaw and forced more peas from their pod. "Majet going?"

The pip looked up, and with eyes, and hands he communicated that he wanted nothing to do with finding the god. He pointed at his mouth as if to say that the god was responsible for the loss of his tongue.

Dar'ock wagged a hand at them. "No. No. I'm not saying that you have to go with me. The two of you can stay here and keep the place up. It's your home as much as mine."

Garfe spilled another run of peas on the floor. "But Garfe Dar'ock's guide dog. Garfe can't let Dar'ock go off alone. Dar'ock need Garfe."

"Garfe, you're civilized now. You're what civilized people call a friend. You're not my dog anymore."

Majet nodded vigorously.

Garfe gave Dar'ock a blank look. He still wasn't quite sure what the word friend meant, though he sensed it was something good.

Dar'ock cocked an eyebrow, and grinned broadly. "Besides, Garfe, civilized or not, I'm sure you have no desire to go to the Hidden City, a place filled with sons of Seth. This valley suits you better."

Garfe wrinkled his brow. "Dar'ock foolish for going off looking for the god."

"So be it, Garfe. So be it."

Dar'ock took out his silver pipe. Garfe looked at Majet, and Majet rolled his eyes and nodded toward the door.

At first light Dar'ock headed out to where Ebony was stabled. Garfe followed close, still trying to dissuade him. Something dark passed overhead. Dar'ock's face went grim. His eyes tracked the blur to a nearby stand of trees. "The raven!" he grated to himself. He could not see the bird for the shadows, but the unwelcome visitor filled the morning air with noise that sounded like mocking laughter. Garfe seemed oblivious to the bird, ignoring its call.

"Persistent," said Dar'ock. "But he hasn't gotten me yet."

Garfe cast Dar'ock a questioning glance.

"Yennea claimed she knew the god," said Dar'ock, ignoring Garfe's confusion. "But the pitiable child never had a life! And poor untainted little Lamar. How could Yennea's god be good and let a child come from the womb gripped in the awful claws of the Death Angel? Like I said,

Garfe, I want answers. And I am going to get them."

"The god might get angry with Dar'ock and add curses," mocked Garfe. He thrust a claw at Dar'ock and added, "Or maybe he tear Dar'ock's heart out, or kill Dar'ock with his breath."

Dar'ock laughed. He cinched Ebony's saddle, and set his foot to the stirrup. He looked over his shoulder at Garfe. "Well, my friend, in that case I shall not return, and this wonderful valley will be yours and Majet's. So how about that!"

"Not funny," growled Garfe. "Garfe always thought Dar'ock clever, but Dar'ock not clever. He dumb to go looking for the god. But Garfe clever. Garfe stay here in nice valley. Majet's lips say words with no sound. Majet tell Garfe, 'the god be cursed.' Garfe agree with Majet. Garfe want nothing to do with the god you seek."

Dar'ock nodded. "The two of you have chosen your course, and I have chosen mine." He swung up into the saddle. It took more effort than he had expected. "I have enjoyed the easy life too long, Garfe. I don't have the strength or quickness I once had."

Garfe smiled, and reached up and touched the scar on the side of his head. Dar'ock grinned. "That's another reason for not taking you with me. Slow as I'm getting, why, I might lose an ear some dark night. Take care, Garfe."

Before Garfe could answer, Dar'ock turned Ebony and galloped away. Dar'ock didn't see the tear that made a line down Garfe's cheek. "The god will not like Dar'ock's questions!" he muttered. Poger, who watched with his head draped over the log fence, nickered as if expressing agreement.

*T*he five-month journey north took an unexpectedly heavy toll on Dar'ock's energy. The trek from the Valley of Bitterness to the gates of the Hidden City left him exhausted. His black coat hung too loose. A scruffy beard shadowed his gaunt face. Eyes sunk deep in their sockets looked through the gate into the bustling city. Dar'ock sighed. He had no desire to mingle with the crowds, but he did look forward to a good meal, and a night's rest. He touched heels to Ebony's flanks, and entered the city. People stared as he passed. "Impudent fools!" He rasped. But the clomp of Ebony's hooves on the cobbled stones and the noise of the city absorbed his mutterings, though not his glare. But still, the passers-by did not turn their eyes aside.

Dar'ock rode past a scattering of hovels just inside the massive outer wall. He passed through a second lesser wall that appeared to have been built for the sole purpose of isolating the impoverished from those who had means. The houses of the patricians were orderly and well kept. He trotted past several nameless buildings, *warehouses*, he presumed.

He came to a building with an engraved wooden sign, Mahalel's Livery. Beyond the stable were a leather goods shop and a mercantile. The other side of the mercantile he saw a sign that read "Pamby's Eatery and Inn." A slow smile spread across Dar'ock's face. He turned in at the stable, gave instructions for Ebony's care and wearily made his way to the inn.

When he walked through the door into the commons of the eatery, all eyes turned his way, and everyone drew back, if ever so slightly. Dar'ock smiled and nodded, though inwardly he sneered. "They're shocked at seeing a son of Cain in their fair city," he thought to himself. He tried not to show his weariness as he crossed the room and took the only chair at a small round table in the far corner.

Dar'ock watched the portly waitress as she trundled about chatting with her customers, bringing out their food, and carrying away their dirty dishes. The woman's eyes sparkled, and her smile compelled. "Pamby," he presumed. His next thought was a blunt one. She may be fat, but she's also pretty!

After taking out an arm full of dishes, Pamby returned to the commons, and came strutting his way. She stopped several paces from his table and stared.

"Have you never waited on a son of Cain, woman?" Dar'ock had tired of the gawking.

"Sorry, traveler." Pamby found her smile again. "What can I get ya'?"

Dar'ock ordered a substantial meal. But when it came he found his appetite not as ravenous as he had thought. He picked at the food then shoved it away.

"Something wrong?"

He looked up. Pamby had returned, and stood watching him. Concern wrinkled her brow.

"If the food don't please ya', be glad to replace it with other."

"No, no, the food's fine. I'm just not as hungry as I thought. But I would ask a favor of you."

She eyed him suspiciously. "And what might that be?"

"I have traveled far looking for one they call Methuselah. Can you tell me where I can find him?"

"Looks like you started your journey a month late. The sorry old man finally got nabbed by the Reaper of Souls day after his 969th birthday. We thought he'd never die. Even took bets on the date of his demise. Haren, over by the door took the winnin's."

"Sorry old man?" Curiosity warped Dar'ock's face. "Was Methuselah not a follower of the god?"

"That he was, traveler," huffed the fleshy bar maid. "And that were his problem. Always tellin' folks what they should and shouldn't be doin'. He could spoil a body's fun afore it ever got started. Why, if'n he could a' pulled it off he would'a even outlawed ale brew and whores."

Dar'ock laughed. But his laughter rang hollow. Deep inside he felt disappointed that he would not get to talk with the old man. He had come so far. Pamby started to walk away, but he regained her attention with a wave of a pale hand. She shifted her weight from one hip to the other "Yea?" she grunted.

"Tell me, Pamby, is there anyone else in town who is a follower of the god?"

"Posh! If there were, you wouldn't want ta know 'em, Son a' Cain." Pamby gave him a wink, put her hands to her hips and shook her head. "Well, traveler, take it yer done wi' yer meal."

Dar'ock nodded. Pamby stepped closer, leaned out and grabbed his plate, gave him a look of disgust, apparently for not having eaten more, and lumbered off to the kitchen. Dar'ock finished his brew, and paid for his meal along with a night's lodging, though Pamby didn't seem particularly pleased to have him. Climbing the stairs took the last of his strength. "Rest. I do need some rest," he mused aloud, as he labored down the hall. His was the last room on the right.

Dar'ock entered, shut the door behind him, and flopped down on the rickety bed. And wobbly though it was, he thought it a sight better than the hard ground. He took out his silver pipe, and quietly played a tune that expressed his inner torment. But the dirge was brief.

Still wrapped in his black coat, Dar'ock lay looking at the cobwebbed ceiling, wondering whether he should continue his quest or return to the Vale of Mourning. "If I continue the quest, where do I go from here?" he mumbled. "Yennea said if you are truly looking for the god you can find him anywhere. She said he is everywhere near. But how can such a thing be? Surely the god cannot be found in a dive like this?"

A tear escaped the corner of Dar'ock's eye. He sighed and rasped, "God, where are you? I would have words with you, god!" He listened. He could hear the noise of laughter down in the commons. Footsteps in the hall. The creak of a door. The wind rattling the window pane. He glanced out the window. Dark clouds moiled across the city. "In the midst of clamor, all I hear is silence." He grated his teeth. "I thought as much."

The sun slipped off to its place taking the light of day with it. Dar'ock stared into the darkness.

"The mark of my life," he sighed.

Chapter 12
Dreadful Dreams

And the God said, "My spirit will not strive with man forever, for man is indeed flesh, and his days are numbered!" The Book of Beginnings

*T*he night lengthened. Dar'ock tossed and turned on his bed until at last he fell asleep. In his restless slumber he dreamed. In his dream, Yennea ran toward him across a flowered meadow. Her golden curls danced on the breeze and her unbridled laughter filled the air. She stopped as if suddenly aware of his presence. She looked at him. Her face turned somber. Her voice came as an echo down a long corridor. "Dar'ock, do you still seek the God?"

His own voice rang hollow. "I called to him. I told him I would have words with him. But as I suspected he was nowhere to be found."

Yennea's childlike laughter echoed off unseen walls. "Oh, Dar'ock, God is not a man to be commanded at one's whim. He is God, Dar'ock. He is greater than princes or kings. Would you acknowledge a man who would come in such a manner seeking audience with you? I think not. But Dar'ock, God truly is everywhere near." Yennea's eyes sparkled as she laughed. She turned and ran back across the meadow. She stopped again, looked over her shoulder, and called out to him. "He is even there at Pamby's

Place." Her face turned away, and she ran off toward the horizon.

Dar'ock ran after her. "Yennea come back!" he cried. But she continued on, as if in slow motion. But still, he could not catch up to her. "I am sorry Yennea! Please forgive me! Please..." She passed from view, but Dar'ock ran on across the seemingly endless tract scattered with blue, purple, orange, red, and yellow flowers.

The flowers suddenly began to grow larger and larger, until he found himself drowning in a sea of color. Then the blue and purple blooms faded, and he found himself surrounded by orange, red, and yellow flowers that swayed in the warm breeze. The warm breeze became a hot wind, and the flowers became dancing flames. Someone screamed.

Through the flames Dar'ock saw the face of the enchantress. Her cries of terror mutated to laughter. Dar'ock became angry when he realized she was laughing at him. Enraged, he ran toward her through the fire, silver dagger in hand. The laughter grew louder, and seemed to come from the flames themselves.

The flames became living creatures with terrible yellow orbs that stared and flashed with malice. With long blazing arms, the fire creatures threw flaming darts at him. From somewhere in the distance he heard Deva's laughter.

He looked and saw her standing beyond the burning creatures, but try as he might he could get no closer to her. The creatures repelled him. Their blazing darts splattered on his naked flesh like hot grease. His dagger melted from his hand.

He looked for a place to flee for refuge, but could no longer see past the flames that engulfed him. And Deva's fiendish laughter that rang like the squawking of a raven battered him. He covered his ears, fell to his knees, and screamed for mercy.

Dar'ock woke in a cold sweat, wet eyes peering into darkness. Wind still rattled the window. There was a flash of light, followed by a loud cracking sound that shook the inn. Dar'ock's sense of dread intensified. He wiped his brow, struggled out of bed, lit a candle, and went to the washbasin. He cooled his face with a handful of water. When Dar'ock looked up, he saw his face reflected in the dusty metal mirror that hung above the basin. He swiped away the gatherings, and his mouth dropped open with horror at the gaunt cheeks, deep eye sockets, and lifeless eyes that stared back at him.

He had seen such a visage before, in little Lamar's face, and before that in Deva's. "The face of death!" he acknowledged to himself, and the admission shook him. "So that's why I feel so weak, and why my clothes hang loose from my shoulders. No wonder people gawk and draw back from me."

His head drooped. He stared down at the basin. "I wonder how long...how long I will live?" He turned away, took off his coat and tossed it on a chair, made his way back to the bed, turned back the blanket, and wilted to a sitting position. He blew out the candle, and sat on the edge of the bed staring into the night.

"God, I do believe you are here. And I don't blame you for not showing yourself to me. Why should you?" he stammered. The words he spoke did not come easily. "Oh, God, I am loathe to admit it, but I am afraid of death."

A deep, resonant voice spoke from the darkness. "But die you shall." Dar'ock dropped to his knees.

"You desire to have words with me." There was power in the voice, but not anger. Dar'ock cautiously lifted his face toward the source of the voice. Darkness had fled, and before him stood a man with hair as silver as his pipe, skin smooth as worn leather, eyes deep and filled with understanding, and a kind face that flashed a beckoning smile. The visitant wore a robe the color of the sky.

For the first time in his life Dar'ock felt small and insignificant. Shame for all of his selfishness, for his wicked thoughts and deeds suddenly weighed heavy, and his mind began to scold him. "You violated Yennea, stole away her smile, and carelessly took her life. Because of your lust, little Lamar came into the world with death on his face. You have hurt so many people over the years."

Tears coursed down Dar'ock's sallow cheeks, and he cried aloud, "Oh God, I am a wicked man. I am not worthy of your presence. I beg you to forgive me! Please, forgive me!"

"I do forgive you, Dar'ock." The God reached out and touched him, and Dar'ock felt strangely different. "The sacrifice I will provide cleanses you of all your transgressions."

"Does that mean I will live?" Hope sprang to life in Dar'ock's voice.

A tear fell from God's eye. He shook his head. "No, Dar'ock, you will not live. You are forgiven, but the nature of life is that you reap what you sow. By your own doing the death is upon you. And dying you shall surely die. But take comfort in this, Dar'ock, you will find death a doorway to another world. You will close your eyes here in the Hidden City, and open them again in the City of the God."

"So be it." The words escaped Dar'ock's lips in a whisper, and without protest.

"And know this Son of Cain, you shall fare better than those among whom you dwell. The world has embraced wickedness like a man bedding his neighbor's wife. I will endure man's iniquity no longer. Judgment is decreed. And so all life shall be destroyed, save Methuselah's great grandson and his family. They alone, with a remnant of the animal kingdom, shall be saved. Yet, Dar'ock, Son of Cain, rest assured, before my deluge has swept this city from the sand on which it is built, you shall be with me in my city."

"Yennea and Lamar?" Dar'ock swallowed hard, and looked at the floor.

"They await your arrival."

"And what of Garfe and Majet?"

Dar'ock thought he heard a mournful sigh. He looked up, but his bleary eyes gaped into darkness. And somewhere in the distance he heard a raven giving angry protest. Dar'ock wept, crawled into bed, and sought for sleep.

Chapter 13
Ol' Noah Was Right

And the God said, "I am bringing a flood of waters upon the earth, to destroy from beneath the heavens all flesh in which is the breath of life." The Book of Beginnings

*T*he next morning Dar'ock shambled down to the commons for breakfast. He ignored the rude stares. Pamby lumbered over and took his order, then shuffled off to the kitchen. She returned with his meal and a stein of hot broth and herbs. "This'll perk ya."

"Say, Pamby, where might I find Methuselah's great grandson?" Dar'ock put the question to her as he lifted the elixir to his lips.

"Noah?" she squawked. "Weird fellow, that one! Word has it he claims the end a' the world is a comin'."

Dar'ock ran his hand through his hair. "Well, strange things last night."

"Ya mean the flashes of light an cracklin' a the sky? Rattled the windows, that's fer sure!"

Dar'ock nodded.

Pamby shrugged her shoulders. "Don't mean nothin ta me. Leastwise not the ruination a' the whole a' what is."

Pamby laughed uncomfortably, but in spite of her attempt at gaiety her eyes spoke fear. Dar'ock took his cup and stared pensively into the bitter brew. "Does this Noah live here in the city?"

"No, he dwells out on the Plains of Jared off west a' here." Pamby gave Dar'ock a dark scowl. "Word has it he's done built himself a huge boat right out in the middle a nowhere. And that, without a lake, sea, or even a small pond anywhere in sight! If ya ask me, the fellow has cracked his egg fer sure."

"Does sound strange, but who knows?" Dar'ock sipped the brew then sat the steaming stein back down on the table. He leaned back in his chair and muttered, "Perhaps Noah is right."

Pamby frowned, mumbled something about madness, waved a hand over her head, and trundled off to *take care of business*.

When his food came, Dar'ock had no appetite for it. Still, he forced himself to eat a few bites. And after a glowering Pamby took his plate he trudged down the street to the stable.

"Ebony, you have served me well. But my time draws to an end, and I will ride you no more. Farewell, old friend."

He sold horse and trappings to the stable master, and returned to Pamby's place, called her aside to where the other patrons would not overhear their conversation. Grim faced, he handed her the silvers he had just received from the stable master. Pamby's eyes went wide, and the corners of her mouth turned down. "What? You want me to send ya one a' my girls tonight?"

Dar'ock understood Pamby's frown. He shook his head. "No, none would be willing. And besides, I have no need for one of your molls. The silver is room rent. I plan to stay on here, Pamby."

"Stay on? Indefinitely?" Her tone rejected his request, but Pamby was a practical woman. Deep furrows creased her brow as she thumbed the silver pieces from one hand to the other. "Nuff here to cover a year's rent and board. Not that you eat much more than a mouse's portion!" She grimaced and shifted the coins back again.

"Please." There was pleading in his voice. "The death is on me." He spoke louder than he had intended. Pamby's mouth dropped open and she glanced out toward the tables to make sure he had not been heard. She leaned away from him and rasped, "I...I should have known! Not catchin' is it?"

"No. You've nothing to worry about in that regard."

She continued to finger the silvers as if contemplating whether to keep them or give them back and send him on his way.

"The inconvenience won't be for long. Probably just a few weeks." He appealed to her with his eyes. "And so that it won't be any trouble to you, I'll make arrangements with the body planter as soon as we're finished here."

"And you'll take your meals in your room?" she bargained looking over her shoulder toward the commons. He agreed, and then wearily plodded off in search of the body planter. He figured his silver dagger would cover the cost.

Two days later Dar'ock awoke feeling nauseous. Pamby brought him his breakfast. He nibbled at it, and after a bit pushed it aside. He retched several times that day, and when evening came he broke out in the sweats. For the next three days he ran a low fever, and ate nothing. Pamby checked on him twice a day. From the look on her face he figured it was not so much out of concern for his welfare, as to determine whether or not it was time to send for the body planter. Having the death at work under her roof seemed to set Pamby on edge. Dar'ock understood her anxiety. If one of her patrons found out...well, the rumors would empty the place. He was quite certain that as far as she was concerned the sooner he died the better.

By the fourth day Dar'ock was so weak he could hardly lift his hand to his brow to wipe away the sweat that dripped down and stung his eyes. He took out his silver pipe, but could bring forth no music. The effort caused his stomach to turn, but there was nothing left to heave. He felt ghastly, but suffered no actual pain.

That night Pamby came into the room with candle in hand, held it over his face and peered down at him. His breathing was labored. She plucked the silver pipe from his chest, and stuck it in her pocket. Dar'ock had no strength to resist. Pamby gaped at him with disdain, and shook her head. "Still with us, huh? Well, I reckon ya won't be with us fer long. Not much left but bones" She leaned closer. "Humph, I know the death rattle when I hear it. May as well send fer the spader."

Pamby turned to leave the room. As she did there was a rumbling sound, and the floor shifted beneath her. Pamby stumbled and nearly dropped the candle. "What the..." White light flashed as it had the night Dar'ock arrived, and the ear splitting crash that followed rattled the window. "Unusual, for sure!" cried Pamby. She caught her breath, and put a hand to her chest and gasped, "Now, now, girl, the doin's out there may rattle yer house, but you musn't let 'em rattle yer head!"

She turned her gaze to Dar'ock and he saw fright in her eyes. He tried to tell her to cry out to the God, but his whisper was lost to the howling wind. The building shuddered again. Pamby's hands flayed the air, and she legged it for the door. The next spasm of the earth caused the inn to buckle. The floor cracked and popped, and hurled her back across the room. She landed on top of Dar'ock, and let out a blood-curdling scream. The candle splatted against the wall and went out. And as if in response, lightning again lit the world. Thunder followed. And on its heels came another roll of the earth. The building shuddered more violently than before. Pamby tumbled off Dar'ock asprawl on the floor.

"Tis' the end a' the world!" she shrieked. "Ol' Noah was right! We'll be swallowed alive for sure!" Pamby scrambled to her feet and fled the room.

Water fell from the heavens. At first the drops drummed soothingly on roof and pane in concert with the wind. Then lightning split the sky again. A powerful clap of thunder quavered Dar'ock's bones, and the rain became a deafening torrent. Dar'ock closed his eyes, a tear escaped the corner. "Oh, Garfe," he groaned, "what will become of you, my friend?"

Dar'ock wept. A slight smile creased his lips. He could see Garfe's earless face, and his bright eyes. He could smell the mustiness of Garfe's hairy body. When Dar'ock thought about the *civilized* Garfe he wanted to laugh, but could not. A peal of thunder brought him back to reality.

Dar'ock sighed deeply. His countenance fell. "What will become of me?" he wondered. He opened his eyes, and looking out into darkness recalled to mind the words God had spoken to him, "Son of Cain, rest assured, before my deluge has swept this city from the sand on which it is built, you shall be with me in my city." His colorless lips slowly twisted into a smile. He let his eyes slip shut. "Peace at last," he whispered.

Lightning not only tore the fabric of the sky, but seemed to rip the crust of the earth. Waters gushed upward to meet the rains pouring down. The earth quaked with brutal force. Screams could be heard throughout the city. The colossal city walls cracked, crumbled, and came crashing down as the rising flood swirled about them. At that same moment the nearby mercantile split into two pieces and tumbled into a fissure. And as the earth convulsed yet again the livery shifted into splinters. The powerful quake broke Pamby's Place at its seams. The Inn collapsed. The waters drenched Dar'ock's body now buried in a heap of rubble. And as the waters that gushed from the soul of the earth joined the waters that fell from above, cries of terror could be heard throughout what had been the Hidden City. But soon the cries fell silent. The rain fell for forty days and forty nights, until the whole earth was covered with water. Only Noah and his family escaped the deluge.

So as judgment fell on a world of men who had corrupted themselves before God, Dar'ock passed the veil of death, and came out into joy, for Dar'ock, a son of Cain, found grace in the eyes of God.

-0-

Thank you for reading this Realms of Light book. How many stars would you give it? Please consider returning to Amazon, rating this book, and writing a brief review.

ABOUT THE AUTHOR

John, a graduate of Appalachian Bible College and Berean Christian College, was born in Battle Creek, Michigan, and grew up in East Leroy, a small town south of Battle Creek. He was an Athens High School All-State, All-American football standout. He served in the Army as a noncommissioned officer during the Viet Nam War era. John is an ordained minister who has experience as a pastor, youth pastor, Christian school teacher, assistant mission director, and mission director. He has been writing Christian fantasy fiction since his two sons were knee high to a gnome. He was a member of a sci-fi fantasy writer's group in Seattle for twelve years, and for three years led a Christian writer's group in Pahrump, NV, a sprawling town in the Mojave Desert where he lives with his wife, Sue.

Other Realms of Light Books

Nonfiction
The God Question
Unveiling John's Vision
Reflections of a Searching Soul
Mentoring Men in Ministry (e-book only)

Fiction (Paperback and e-book formats)
Accidental Heroes series:
The Helot – Book One
Dark Danger – Book two
Terminus – Book three
Primal Blade – Book four
Acceptable Fruit
Imagine Christmas
Once Upon a Knight
Phantom Island Chronicles
Son of Cain
Tales of a Church Mouse
The Droll Child
The Jewel
The Myth
The Princess and the Orc
Wanzalara's Cottage
Word of Honor
Unlikely Heroes
The Requiting (Framer of Times series: book 1)

Deliverance (e-book only)
Journey to the Tower of Death (e-book only)
Moon Drale (e-book only)
Tarnished Crown (e-book only)

REALMS OF LIGHT BOOKS

website
Johnedgell-author.com

email
Jaedgell.author@gmail.com

Made in the USA
Columbia, SC
10 September 2022